My Summer of Southern Discomfort

My Summer of Southern Discomfort

STEPHANIE GAYLE

WILLIAM MORROW *An Imprint of* HarperCollins*Publishers*

Grateful acknowledgment is made to reprint excerpts from "I Know an Old Lady Who Swallowed a Fly." Words by Rose Bonne. Music by Alan Mills. Copyright © 1952, 1954 by Peer International Corporation. Copyright renewed. International copyright secured. Used by permission. All rights reserved. All rights administered by Peer International Corporation.

HarperCollins books may be purchased for educational, business, or sales promotional use. For information please write: Special Markets Department, HarperCollins Publishers, 10 East 53rd Street, New York, NY 10022.

FIRST EDITION

Designed by Susan Yang

Library of Congress Cataloging-in-Publication Data

Gayle, Stephanie, 1975–
My summer of southern discomfort/Stephanie Gayle.—1st. ed.
p. cm.
ISBN: 978-0-06-123629-7
ISBN-10: 0-06-123629-2
1. Women lawyers—Fiction. 2. Self-realization—Fiction. 3. Georgia—Fiction.
I. Title.

PS3607.A98576M9 2007
813'.6—dc222 2006052147

07 08 09 10 11 JTC/RRD 10 9 8 7 6 5 4 3 2 1

To C.S.L.,

for setting me on the path

ACKNOWLEDGMENTS

Many thanks to all those who nurtured this novel and me during its creation: you are brave, kind people. Special karma is owed to Beth Gallagher and Ann Sheybani for lending me their writing wisdom and editing prowess; Bill Reiss, my agent and angel; Carolyn Marino, my splendid editor; Julie Iatron for superior cheerleading and the promise of Girl Scout sales skills; and my parents, especially Mom, who gave me the title.

Chapter One

March 11, 2000

"I don't know why she swallowed the lye," the boy sings, emphasis on "don't." He slips the yellow package of bubble gum into his pocket too fast, then tilts his head up and smiles at me, teeth bright against his dark skin. Cute little thief.

"Dominic," his mother whispers. "What all are you doing?" She brushes raindrops from her tight, glossy curls.

"Practicing my magic trick." He returns the gum to its candy tray slot.

Good story, I think. Here in Georgia it is classified misdemeanor theft by shoplifting. I consider sentencing. A five-dollar fine? Community service?

His mother tells me, "He wants to be a magician this week." Anxious to assure me her son is no career criminal.

Unperturbed, he loads a bottle of juice onto the conveyor belt while singing, "I don't know why she swallowed the lye. I guess she'll die."

The supermarket smells of damp overcoats and soil. "This wet will help," the cashier says. "Before today it was so dry the trees were bribing the dogs." I tilt my head to the side and consider her comment. Oh. Ha. Will I ever understand this honeyed speech in real time?

Dominic tries to lift a heavy bag of potatoes from the depths of the cart. "I don't know why she swallowed the lye." He lets dramatic tension build before singing, "I guess she'll diiiiiieeeee!"

His mother shooshes him while keeping her eyes focused on the automated scanner.

As he swings into the third verse his mother absentmindedly remarks in that mysterious way that reveals how maternal brains are focused on their children at all times, "Baby, it's fly, not lye. Fly."

No, no, I want to tell him. "Fly" doesn't make any sense. Who dies from swallowing a fly? No one. If swallowing flies was fatal, think how many motorcyclists would litter our highways! But lye makes sense. Lye is a poisonous substance. Swallowing it might kill the old lady. Although then the song would have only one verse.

I unload my small basket, careful not to touch the white plastic divider that separates my single-sized servings from Dominic's family's bulk containers of rice, beans, potatoes, orange juice, bananas, and deli meats. I forget I no longer live in the Northeast where such trespasses incur stricter punishments.

I place a container of low-fat peach yogurt on the conveyor belt and consider that maybe it is not lye after all but lie. What if the old lady swallowed a lie? Now there exists the basis for a multiple-versed song. Perhaps she swallowed a lie about someone's guilt and the police came to interview her and she had to go to court. I sing the song inside my head as I set my basket on the linoleum floor, on top of a discarded weekly with articles devoted to the upcoming Southern Belle Ball.

Dominic and his mother walk behind their bag-laden cart. It squeaks toward the automatic doors that will whoosh open and consume them and their song. I glance out the tall, fingerprint-smudged windows, checking to see if the rain has lessened.

"I don't know why she swallowed the lie."

A dark car drives past and I can feel my forehead tighten as I squint, trying to see if its license plate is blue and white. The falling rain obscures it. I contort my neck; adjust my stance, lean forward. Blue and white? White and blue? Which is it?

The car is gone before I can decide. Not that it matters. It's not him. I should know better.

The grocery clerk clears her throat again to get my attention. I mutter "sorry" and give her the money displayed on the register total. The grocery bag has a grinning pig face on it. "Keep dry now," the clerk calls after me.

The puddle-spotted parking lot is almost empty. I curl my toes inside my damp sneakers and try to think of a different song to sing. No use dwelling on the lies I swallowed that led me here, to the Piggly Wiggly parking lot in Macon, Georgia. No use wondering if swallowed lies ever dissolve or if they remain forever hard, like rocks. After a moment, I move toward my car and begin whistling "Oh, Susannah" because it is the first song I think of, it sounds cheerful, and it means nothing to me at all.

Chapter Two

June 26, 2000

My corkscrew curls, inching upward and outward, each wiry strand like the fiber of a freshly severed rope, tell me that today will be hot and wet, again.

The iron emits baby-dragon puffs of steam that make my hair frizz worse as they smooth the creases from my pants. Erasing lines with the iron's hot metal face is a little magical. Now you see it, now you don't. Comparing laundering to magic would secure my reputation as an organizational freak among my colleagues at the district attorney's office. They see my tidy office and pristine wardrobe as symptoms of an obsessive-compulsive disorder. If only they knew that I once possessed a life plan, taking me from years fifteen to sixty-five, and that, until a year ago, I followed that plan without deviation.

The phone rings and my hand shakes, creating a wrinkle near the belt line. Silly. I bet it's Carl calling from the office to confirm that I will be in court at two o'clock, as if I need reminding.

I pick up the white cordless receiver.

"Natalie?" a male voice asks. Carl. His anxious drawl is inimitable. Before meeting him I did not believe a born-and-bred Georgian could sound jittery while maintaining the slow, thick cadence of Southern speech. He tells me that Ben called in sick and wants to know if I can handle the Biddle deposition. A tap-tapping informs me that he is engaged in the nasty habit of hitting a pencil against his teeth. The sound makes the dark hairs on my forearms rise.

"Certainly. I will be in soon." I hang up before he can respond. It takes two minutes to finish my ironing, the tiny wrinkle I made near the belt line now a mere memory. If only all mistakes were so easily erased.

I grab my leather satchel and pause to recheck that the iron is off and I have all I need: wallet, memos, apple, latest death threat, bills to be mailed. I scoop my keys from the yellow ceramic bowl in the narrow front hall. The bowl was my mother's suggestion for putting an end to my days of mislaid keys. This foolproof system represents one of the few things I have adopted from my mother.

From my father, I took almost everything: his brown eyes, his small ears, his profession, his tenacity, and his name, Goldberg. I am Natalie Goldberg. My father is Aaron Goldberg, the famous civil rights lawyer. When people discover I am a lawyer they assume I am following my father's path, until I inform them that I work for the district attorney. "You mean you work to put people away?" Yes. I work to put people away.

Outside the sun is strong and the air covers me like a damp towel. Atop my front steps I tilt my face skyward and close my eyes. A red disk hovers in the reversed negative background behind my lids. The scent of my next-door neighbor's gardenias tickles my nose. I open my eyes, adjust my sunglasses, and advance into another Monday, prepared to do battle on behalf of Bibb County, Georgia.

The district attorney's offices are on Mulberry Street, just beyond the Grand Opera House, a century-old gem where Houdini and Charlie Chaplin once performed. Inside our lobby, the security guard, George, nods as I walk past. He will nod at me on my way out, assuming I am done with work before his shift ends at seven P.M.

On days less humid than this I take the stairs because the elevator is a death trap. When I push the gold button marked three it rumbles to life and shakes until it reaches the third floor where it collapses with a groan. Since I began working here ten months ago I have asked repeatedly when the elevator will be replaced. My queries have met with incredulous looks, laughter, and the occasional sympathetic "Not until someone dies."

Hannah, the new receptionist of the five-inch nail extensions, hands me two pink message slips and says, "Morning." She does not offer an opinion on whether the morning is good or not. That isn't in her job description.

The day sounds like any other: phones beeping, papers chug-chugging out of the copier, someone saying, "Wait. Just a minute. He did *what*?" It smells like an intern burned the coffee again. I pass through the hall, not stopping to call out morning greetings as others do, and head for my office. It once belonged to a popular, now retired lawyer everyone refers to as "Guvnor," though he never held a political office. The furniture inside—a massive maple desk and an imposing matching chair—makes me look Lilliputian. I could have exchanged the pieces, but I refused, sensing the action would label me a prima donna.

The furniture is the only thing with personality in the room. No photographs disturb the order of my desk. My degrees from Smith and Harvard remain in storage. Anyone entering my office would be hard-pressed to identify its owner. It could belong to anyone, or rather, to no one.

I turn the lights and air-conditioning on and shrug my linen jacket off. I reach, tiptoe, to hang it on the closet door hook, to preserve its wrinkle-free state for my court appearance and the absent Ben's deposition. I search my desk for his paperwork.

A knock on my open door draws my gaze to William Brown, district attorney. He wears a pin-striped three-piece suit that belongs on an older white man. Will, the youngest and only black DA in the city's history, has enough to battle without adding fashion worries to his list. He stands on my threshold holding a sheaf of papers. "Looking for these?"

"If that is Ben's deposition, yes. If it is anything else, no."

He hesitates before asking, "You okay? Not feeling overloaded, are you? I can assign Ben's deposition to Carl."

My head is shaking "no" before he has finished. "No, I'm fine." I extend my hand for the papers. He steps forward and relinquishes them.

"I know things have been tough since Jeffrey left."

I make a noise, signaling agreement, but not loudly enough to be considered complaint.

Jeffrey Barr mentored me during my first months here. He quit five weeks ago. The office gossipmongers are still speculating. Some say he left because he was not nominated for Will's position, others say his marriage was on the rocks, and there is always the argument that, after twelve years, he burned out. Whatever the reason, Jeffrey left, and the rest of us are scrambling to take on extra cases.

Will's hazel eyes search my room. "It occurs to me that you haven't taken any vacation since you arrived. Summertime can be a bit quiet around here, what with all the judges golfing." He smiles and I smile in return because he is my boss. "If you want to take some time off, we can reshuffle your caseload. Maybe give you a chance to finally unpack your things." He stares at my bare walls.

"Thanks. I'll think about it." He nods, and begins to leave but stops. What now?

"Natalie, I don't think I've told you how pleased I am that you joined our office. I still don't understand why you sacrificed a position at a major Manhattan law firm for this low-paying support position"—a silence extends, a pause I could fill with explanations but don't, as usual—"but I'm grateful that you did. You met a sharp learning curve and handled it beautifully." He stares at the large chair I half hide behind. "I think Guvnor would be proud," he says, earning a small but honest smile from me.

"Thank you, Will." I want to say more but my tight throat won't let any more words past.

"No, *thank you,*" he says before leaving, gazing at a space filled with Guvnor's furniture and little else.

I sit and rub my index finger over my right eyebrow. A quiet, dry laugh escapes me. Poor Will, still wondering why I chose to abandon the fast track of corporate law for public prosecution work. Many times I have explained that I never wanted to pursue corporate law. He keeps asking why, in indirect ways. Somehow Will has sussed out that I am not telling the whole truth and nothing but the truth.

I rub my sweaty palms against the cool wooden desk. The truth would destroy hope of further comparisons to good old Guvnor. Coming to Macon was not motivated by a desire to change career tracks. It was the result of a disastrous love affair.

My honesty about not wanting to work in corporate law is unimpeachable. I aspired to civil rights law, my father's field. I sought to expand its reach to foreign soil, to apply a higher standard to international human rights, to make the world a better place. Three years at Harvard Law wasn't enough to knock the ideological stuffing out of me. Still, no one offered me the position of "improver of the human condition" upon graduation. When the offers came in, I found myself faced with a decision. I could work for a national nonprofit organization I was less committed to or I could work for the bad guys, defenders of capitalist wealth, who offered me outrageous salaries and benefits for my overeducated mind.

My father urged me to work at Walters, MacLittle, and Tate. Their reputation was the best and they had recently instituted pro bono work, requiring it of new associates. I could do good-guy stuff on the side. No matter that they only did so to refute accusations that they had been less willing to contribute to the city's supply of pro bono lawyers than any other large firm.

Dad's blessing, combined with a spreadsheet that revealed that working there for four years would allow me to pursue my dream job financially unhindered, made signing the cream vellum letter of acceptance easier. Even the life plan I had created allowed for a five-year span of work unrelated to human rights law. I was still pursuing the dream.

Working at Walters, MacLittle, and Tate, I noticed three things immediately: I was one of fifteen female lawyers in a stable of one hundred and fifty lawyers; no one at the firm referred to President Bill Clinton without sneering; and everyone played golf. Mars could not have been more surreal.

My first nine months were spent working seventeen-hour days broken only by bathroom visits and meals eaten at my desk. In my small cell I reviewed figures and reread contracts, trying to spot loopholes through which our clients could be divested of some of their billions of dollars. Then, one day, an associate's appendix ruptured. His caseload included an upcoming SEC investigation of a client. I was told to meet with the supervising lawyer, Henry Tate, immediately.

Henry was *the* Tate, the third partner of the firm and the youngest. His hair was gray, but he had an athlete's body. By the few wrinkles on his face I judged him to be forty-six. He laughed as he shook my hand. He gestured me to sit before asking, "Expecting someone older?"

I apologized, mentally berating myself for my transparent expression.

"No need. Now if you had expected someone younger, why then I might ask for the apology you so kindly offered." He didn't tell me his age then; I later learned it to be fifty-two.

His ease, his humor, and his good will comforted me. In that place where few people spoke to me except to ask if I had the papers ready yet or if I knew where the blue copy paper was stored, I yearned for human contact as I never had before. Still, Henry Tate wasn't just anyone. I sensed it as he explained the importance of the case before us and of our work on it. As his deep voice continued to expound in multisyllabic legalese I found myself believing his words; that was his gift, his magic. He made you believe, or want to believe. And that was my mistake: falling in love with Henry Tate and his words.

Chapter Three

I am not eager to review the deposition papers Will gave me. Ben, who was handling the case, is my least favorite colleague. I first saw him at the water cooler, discussing opposing counsel. He said, "Helen Leland. You know, the reason God made miniskirts?" Afterward, when I saw his plush head of gray hair bent over a letter or his stout form leaving for court, I thought, "That's Ben Maddox. The reason God made sexual harassment laws." Further interaction with him has done little to improve upon that impression.

I shuffle the papers so all the corners are aligned. Then I begin making preliminary notes in my Black n' Red notebook. When my friend Lacey returned from her postgraduation literary tour of Europe, she gave me a set of London Bridge salt and pepper shakers and a sturdy notebook with a red and black elastic that bound its pages together. "Legal pads are so trite," Lacey said, helping me pack for Harvard. "Dare to be different, darling." She dropped the *r* in "darling" for an elongated "ahh" sound. Marlene Dietrich or maybe Joan Crawford. I have trouble deciphering Lacey's film star impersonations. They all sound alike to me.

I exhale, dazed. Reviewing Ben's work is a novel experience. I feared that reading his notes would be like exploring a dark cave littered with bat excrement and scary half-human grunts. Instead I have stumbled across an underground paradise glittering with uncut gems. "She saw Brown shoot Anderson from her second-floor window. Be sure she demonstrates how close they stood to each other. Have her repeat Brown's words to Anderson: 'You will pay for that.' " He had distilled the elements of the case into brief, clear sentences few lawyers, muddled by years of reading and writing obtuse language, can construct.

Nowhere did I find evidence of the good old boy who routinely quotes the Bible and conservative politicians. No signs of the sexist who calls all women, regardless of age, "little lady."

I put aside the papers and extract my things from my briefcase. Damn. The death threat. I forgot to mention it to Will, and to give it to Hannah for filing. We maintain a file of all threats: death and other. Each has to be reported to the Macon Police Department. Mine arrived Friday evening in my post office box. Addressed to *Natile Goldburg, Atorny, Macon*, the plain white envelope contained a sheet ripped from a spiral-bound notebook. The misspelled note referred to me as a Jew bitch and Nazi racist, a combination that assured me studying history was not the writer's hobby. It came one day after my prosecution of Mr. Arnold Harlen and his sentence to twenty-five years in prison for two counts of armed robbery. My mother told me you can't please everyone, but I didn't believe her. Criminal law has taught me what my mother never could: there is no such thing as a happy compromise.

I set aside the death threat. I don't believe a Harlen family member will kill me. Whoever wrote the note made no attempt to find my unlisted telephone number and address. The letter breached the sanctum of my mailbox only because Macon postal employees care that letters are delivered to the proper address, even when misaddressed. After years of experiencing postal employee indifference, I am more surprised by this dedication than any threatening note.

I extract my laptop from the long, low drawer of the multishelved bookcase behind me. The machine whirls, chirps, and beeps. E-mail comes first. Among the two dozen requests for legal information, notices of trials, and job-related business is a message titled "Word for the day" with Lacey's return address. I open it first.

> Nat,
>
> Have you seen the new *Alumnae Quarterly* yet? Claudia Monroe has a wedding photo inside. She got married in March. To a man! Miss "I'm here, I'm queer, and I'm not going anywhere" donned a white gown and is playing Barbie to some Miami plastic surgeon Ken. So, in honor of Claudia's new straight-girl status, I've coined a new word: heterotory (hĕt'ə-rō-tōrē) n. Meaning: The heterosexual territory explored by persons formerly identified as gay. Example: I wonder how long Claudia's sojourn into heterotory will last?
>
> Care to place a wager?
>
> Love,
>
> Lacey

Should I reply? No. I will call her tonight. I am running behind schedule with Ben's work on my desk.

My Smith education is one of the strikes Ben holds against me. He thinks it remains a home for privileged young women whose families send them to get a little learning until it is time to marry. When I attended, Smith was an ultraliberal campus funded by conservative money. Ben, who is fifty-six and does not know anyone who graduated post-1962, assumes the school has not changed, and so regards me as one of the spoiled "girls with pearls."

My Harvard degree also riles him. Ben attended Mercer University School of Law, just down the road, where, he tells me, he received an education equal to mine. Based on his notes, I am inclined to agree. I wonder if Mercer's faculty does not feel compelled to stuff their students' heads with as many fifty-cent legal terms as possible.

The phone rings. It's Carl. He is tapping his pencil against his teeth again. I grind my teeth in response and assure him that I am handling Ben's deposition and I will be in court to handle Mr. Gaffer's arraignment. If I were paranoid, I would worry about Carl's monitoring of my work. If I were susceptible, I might find his attentions flattering. He is thirty-three, thus age appropriate, and one handsome Gentile: blond hair, blue eyes, and a great smile. Unfortunately, he is plagued by a need to make sure that everything is operating as it should. I cannot remember a time I felt things were operating as they should. Before I came to Macon, certainly, but how long ago?

Chapter Four

Each time I approach the courthouse on Mulberry Street, I remember first seeing it from the half-open window of a cab, as I traveled from the airport to my new house. The passing faces, all brown, my driver's bewildering speech, and the strong perfume of jasmine and barbecuing meats overwhelmed me.

All red brick, windows, and Roman columns, the courthouse guarded the corner of two busy streets. A squat clock tower sat atop the flat roof, covered by a green dome. The rusted Roman numerals on the clock's large face indicated it was almost noon. Stopped at the red light, I watched as the clock's huge wooden hands reached higher. A deep tolling sounded. The cabbie pointed and said something. Not understanding, I followed his pointed forefinger and watched, astonished, as the clock's hands sped forward ten minutes. We drove past and I asked what had just happened. Through hand gestures and repeated words, he made me understand that the wooden hands were too heavy. Their weight caused the clock to run fast at its zenith and slow at the half-hour mark. My back pressed against the cracked navy leather of my seat and I smiled. It was a tiny smile, little more than a grimace, but it was enough. I had come to a place where the weight of a clock's hands prevented it from keeping proper time.

The courthouse is still my favorite building. There are prettier places in Macon—Hay House, Woodruff House, and the whole of downtown when the city's 275,000 Yoshino cherry trees blossom—but the courthouse remains embedded in my memory as the building with the quirk that made me smile on a very hard day. I have since learned that the courthouse, completed in 1924, is Bibb County's fourth.

It used to house prisoners but it was deemed a potential firetrap, so in 1980 a caravan of cop cars led and followed a group of school buses filled with prisoners to their new home in the Bibb County Law Enforcement Center on Oglethorpe. I learned about the transport and courthouse details from court employees and locals who like to share details of Macon's past.

Coming from Cambridge, Massachusetts, I had ingested a steady diet of Pilgrims, Indians, and Founding Fathers, and followed the paths of Plimoth Plantation and the Freedom Trail on school trips with mind-numbing regularity. In Cambridge, however, history was treated as the past: a slide show to watch and admire. Here, in Macon, history is a different piece of the present, a little worn at the edges and faded, but still tangible. This living past appeals to me in a way I did not anticipate.

A sense of peace fills me as I ascend steps shadowed by an arched brick entryway. I doubt most people enter the courthouse feeling this way. Sounds bounce from the marble lobby floors and ricochet around the room's high ceiling. I nod to the building employees and attorneys I recognize and stare at those I don't know. Today the lobby is quiet. Will was right about the courthouse schedule slowing down in the summer. Though crimes tend to rise, judges tend to disappear, and so the court calendar fills with hearings and arraignment delays.

Just beyond the lobby, propped against the wall beside the closed doors of Courtroom One stands the scarecrow figure of Detective Wilkins. He taps his cap against his right thigh in a slow, steady rhythm. I advance until I am standing in his long shadow. He looks down. "Hello, Miss Goldberg," he says, his voice cautious but friendly. He doesn't know why I am here. It could be to harass him about evidence he has gathered that I am not satisfied with or it could be to say thank you for work well done. I am here for neither.

"Good afternoon, Detective Wilkins. Testifying today?" His cap tapping makes me think so. Some cops loathe entering that small wooden box and restating facts before judge, jury, and attorneys. Detective Wilkins is one of them. He presents well: an authoritative voice and a temper most defense attorneys find difficult to rile. He does not enjoy it, though.

"Just waiting around for Frank." Frank Cox is his partner, a heavy man with a handlebar moustache and thinning hair. Seen together, Wilkins and Cox look like a mismatched nursery-rhyme couple.

"I won't keep you. Seeing you reminded me that I received a death threat this weekend, so I can have one of the clerks drop it off at the station, or leave it at our front desk for pickup."

"Another one?" His black eyebrows descend into diagonal slashes and his coffee-colored lips purse as if for a kiss. It's his deep-thought look. "Didn't you receive one last month?"

"Yes, but that was related to the Gomes case, and it seemed like a juvenile prank. Your partner thought so," I say, trying to lift his brows back to normal position with my nonchalance. "This one has to do with the Harlen case. Ten to one it's a family member."

"You've gotten popular fast." He stares at me, trying to see what it is about me that prompts people to pen death threats.

"It's the job." I shrug, trying to wiggle out from his gaze. "I'm not worried. It didn't come to my house or anything. Just my post office box, and the person didn't have the number."

"God bless the Macon post office," he mutters. "I'll send someone by for it."

I switch my briefcase from right hand to left. "I'll set it out front after I return to the office."

"Where is it now?"

"On the desk in my office. I forgot to file it with the others this morning."

He sighs, a Lord-grant-me-patience sigh. "Miss Goldberg, you have to treat each threat as if it were real, no matter how silly it may seem." A headshake is followed by, "I bet your parents would be appalled if they knew how casually you treat these letters."

My right foot taps against the marble. "Detective, I am not a child anymore, and if I seem blasé about the threats it may be because I grew up in a house where these sorts of letters filled our mailbox. My father's cases made some people very angry." This is true, although I do not mention that these letters were hidden from me until I was a teenager and that they terrified me with their ugly words promising retribution in blood. I'm trying to establish an "I grew up in the trenches" bravado.

Detective Wilkins falls for it. He nods, his brows level again. "File it as soon as you get back to the office, and I'll send someone to get it." I agree and am prepared to walk away when he adds, "You've a dab of something on your pants."

I look down. A small stain, darker than the gray of my pants, dots my right thigh. It wasn't there this morning. "Shit," I say and then mumble, "Sorry."

"Nice to know you're capable of agitation." His mouth twitches in harmony with his lifted brows.

His tone, his expression, combined with Will's statements of this morning, make me ask, "Does everyone around here think I'm inhuman?" I curse myself as soon as the words are out of my mouth. I don't care what they think.

His smile returns. "Frank thinks you were raised in a convent by lawyers and librarians."

"And you?" Good Lord, why can't I keep my mouth closed?

"Oh, Frank's crazy." I reward him with a smile. "I figure there had to be a couple of marines to help." His quiet laughter colors the tips of my ears red. I walk away before he sees this.

The second floor of the courthouse contains offices and meeting rooms. In one of these rooms the deposition of Mrs. Clay Biddle is to be held. Mary Biddle, who prefers to be called Mrs. Clay Biddle, witnessed a murder twelve days ago. She claims to have seen her neighbor, Nelson Brown, shoot and kill his friend John Anderson. Normally, the attorney the DA assigns to the case would call upon Mrs. Biddle to testify at trial. Unfortunately, Mrs. Biddle is a woman in her late sixties plagued by diabetes and heart complications. She is scheduled to enter the Medical Center of Central Georgia for a triple bypass next week. As the outcome of such an operation is uncertain and Mr. Brown's trial is not scheduled until six weeks later, our office has taken the precaution of deposing Mrs. Biddle before she enters the operating room.

Opposing counsel, in the form of Ms. Helen Leland, "the reason God made miniskirts," is already seated at the table. From her lacquered blond updo to her pale peach suit, Helen proves that there is life after beauty pageants. Miss Georgia 1994 often uses her feminine wiles in court to persuade her victims that she is harmless, just before she mauls them. I have seen her reduce an egotistical pillar of the community to a teary mess in less than ten minutes. I admire her, but the cretins she defends are often so deplorable I question her judgment. These are the type of men who torture fellow humans because they "were just having a little fun."

I nod to Helen and she says "good afternoon" in the same tone that once answered the title-determining question in the 1994 Miss Georgia pageant: "If you could be any flower, which would you be?" Helen's answer: "The Cherokee Rose, because it represents the proud state of Georgia and because its many thorns prove that it is strong while its delicate petals show that it is beautiful. And that's how I like to think of myself: beautiful, strong, and a Georgian through and through." I've seen the tape. She looks younger, wearing a white sequined evening gown, but her flawless smile is the same.

The court clerk and stenographer are present. A small Bible rests on the long wooden table, ready to be used to swear in Mrs. Biddle before her testimony. I rearrange my papers and glance at my watch. It's 12:34 P.M. Helen peeks at my watch, too, not to check the time, for there is a loud, ticking timepiece on the wall. It is the covert stare of a woman examining another woman's jewelry. The watch has an eighteen-karat white gold band and a mother-of-pearl dial, circled by diamonds. A Hanukkah present to myself when last year's watch broke. I upgraded, in a major way. Helen's eyes follow the band as I adjust it.

I stare at Helen's manicured hands and wonder if her shaped oval fingernails are real. My ruminations are cut short by the arrival of Mrs. Biddle. She rushes into the room, wheezing, her sizable bosom straining her black silk dress. The clerk hurries forward to assist her into her seat. I hope she lives long enough to give us her testimony.

After a glassful of water and a few minutes to "compose herself" Mrs. Clay Biddle launches into her tale. She is a good storyteller, the kind we in the DA's office love. She does not embellish unnecessarily or contradict her earlier statement to the police.

She seems to have stepped from the pages of a novel. Over her black silk dress she wears a doilylike shawl. When relating distressing details she presses a violet embroidered handkerchief to her broad mahogany brow. Yet I sense she is a stoic Southern woman. The kind who has buried children and suffered bad husbands and worked two or more shifts and kept body and soul together when weaker humans would give up. Mrs. Biddle triumphs over all, including Helen's many attempts to make her admit that her failing health might have been responsible for misidentifying the accused. She admits that diabetes often impairs people's vision, but says she had her eyes examined two weeks ago.

"My doctor says I still don't need glasses, just a coronary artery bypass grafting operation for three blocked arteries." That puts a stop to Helen's questions about her health.

Helen leaves after the testimony is signed and sealed, no doubt planning her bargaining strategy. She has to know the case against her client is locked. I approach Mrs. Biddle.

"Ain't no thing but a chicken wing." She pats my proffered right hand and smiles at my surprise. During her testimony, she had used very little vernacular. "Don't you worry, butterfly. I know how and when to talk proper."

I tell her the district attorney's office appreciates her civic assistance in this case, and she waves aside my thanks. "I just hope that boy's mother can sleep at night easier. Both boys' mothers. Sometimes losing your own to prison isn't an easy thing, but the right thing."

I walk alongside her downstairs, she on her way home and I to the courtroom for my two P.M. arraignment of Mr. Gaffer for one count of conspiracy to commit murder. She squeezes my hand when we reach the lobby.

"It nearly stopped my ticker seeing two girls waiting for me," she confesses. "I thought I was in the wrong room." Oh no, not another older female who believes women like Helen and me belong in a kitchen chasing a toddler.

"That other lawyer sure was sharp, wasn't she?" she says.

"Knives could take lessons," I agree.

Mrs. Biddle cackles. "You two gonna be all right. Bet you have the men around here"—she glances at the suited and uniformed males nearby—"running scared." I feel the tug in my left cheek that signifies my dimple is on display.

"You take care." I pray that her surgery goes well.

"I'll be just fine, butterfly. Now go give 'em hell." She waves her handkerchief at me.

I square my shoulders and exhale. Showtime.

Chapter Five

I exit the coffee shop with a mocha espresso drink around three o'clock. My postarraignment-hearing caffeine shot, to be savored along with the remand judgment I wrestled out of Judge Thompson. He is known to be liberal in making allowances for the accused, but I took every reasonable objection he, the defendant, and his attorney had and stomped all over them in my two-inch heels. Mr. Michael Gaffer will not be vacating his room at the Bibb County Law Enforcement Center anytime soon.

A large swallow of my drink wraps my taste buds around my twin loves of chocolate and coffee. I am getting better at this legal game. Perhaps I should celebrate by sitting down on a bench and finishing my drink in the out-of-doors.

I look across the street to where two benches are unoccupied. Something on the periphery makes me turn my head. I gasp, choking on my coffee. Henry. He stands outside the hardware store, his face dark with a shadow cast by the store's awning. He is looking in the opposite direction, toward the library. Henry loves libraries.

My drink sloshes in its container and my briefcase bangs against my thigh in rhythm with my hurried steps. Bang, bang, bang.

He has come to apologize, to ask me to forgive him, to explain. I am almost there. Soon I will be on his side of the street, within striking distance. He will smell as he always does, a blend of books and leather and man and bay rum. I ignore a driver's graphic insult as I run in front of his car on the very street where I prosecute others for lawlessness. I narrow my eyes against the afternoon sun. I switch coffee and briefcase to my left hand. My right forms a fist. I will bruise his eyes, both eyes. He turns and the helium leaves my body, for the man I am hurrying toward is not my former lover and boss, but a total stranger. He is tall and gray-haired, yes, but heavier and older and, dear God, balding. My face blooms red as a poppy; I can feel the heat.

"I'm sorry," the man says to me, backing up a step. "Do I know you?"

"No." My head shakes in violent denial. "No, no."

"Oh, I thought perhaps—" Why must he continue? I have to stop him.

"No, I . . . I thought you were someone else, someone I knew. I'm sorry." And I am, far sorrier than he will ever know.

The fake Henry backs up another step. Did he see the fury in my face? Does he know I was about to hit him?

"Sorry," he says, but sounds relieved.

This is not the first time. I have seen other Henries in other places, parking outside the video store, mailing a package at the post office, driving past the grocery.

Nine months ago, while shopping for shampoo, I mistook a man no older than myself for Henry. It was the way he was reading the label on the back of a bottle of hair gel. Henry read everything with fixed attention: flyers, grocery lists, and law briefs. When the young man set the container down to ask, "Miss, are you okay?" his voice was rich and smooth, like caramel, even better than Henry's voice. That was the worst moment. I ran away, afraid to look and see that he was more attractive, as well. I could not bear it, not then. Now I want only to kick him, maim him, wound him, ruin him.

I know he is not coming. It has been almost a year. Why must I spot these imposters?

I toss my three-quarters-full drink in the nearest trash receptacle. My throat feels swollen and the beverage has lost its curative power. My white-knuckled grip on my briefcase renders my hand half numb when I reach my office. I drop it and reach for the death threat, Officer Wilkins's stern warning in my ears. My swiftness in taking it to Hannah owes less to his ire and more to the fact that the letter represents something I can do, now, a task to accomplish. Anything to keep me from thinking of what transpired on the street, my near assault of a stranger.

Hannah takes the envelope with a sniff not symptomatic of a cold.

"Something the matter?" I ask as she turns to look at her phone board, aglow with little red lights representing other people's conversations.

"No," she says, as if I am crazy for asking. "Just seems a lot of people don't like you around here."

I almost ask if she is one of them but I don't. I head for my office where paperwork awaits. You would think it was chocolate the way I hurry toward it.

Chapter Six

"To market to market to buy a fat pig. Home again, home again, jiggety jig." Perhaps it's not the best nursery rhyme for a Jew, but I never kept kosher and I do not know any other homecoming rhymes except for "Ladybug, Ladybug, fly away home" and that involves arson.

The living room glows in the legacy of the late setting sun. My hand hovers over the light switch. The pale blue walls are lavender and the long low coffee table before my sofa shines pink, as if blushing. I swallow as if I could imbibe the stillness and let it settle in my stomach, warm and soft. And then I flip the switch and expose my life to incandescence.

A cricket symphony practices outside the living room windows left open for ventilation. I silence them with the air conditioner. I walk through the house, dropping items into their appropriate places: keys in the bowl, satchel by the front hall, mail on the kitchen counter, peaches in the fruit bowl.

I dial Lacey's number. It rings three times. She is not home or not answering, because it only takes me two rings to reach from one end of Lacey's studio apartment to the other. Maybe one and a half rings for Lacey. She has longer legs. After four rings her machine voice says, "You have reached . . . me. The bad news is I'm not here. The good news is that I hope to be here again sometime. Leave a message. Oh, and if *you* have bad news? Call someone else."

I hang up before the screeching beep ends. I will try her again later.

In the kitchen I consider my dinner options. The phone rings. Did Lacey intuit my need to talk? I close the refrigerator and pick up the phone.

"Hi, sweetheart."

Lacey never calls me "sweetheart" and her voice, bless her, never has this much sunshine in it. She was born in the age of irony, unlike my mother.

"Hi, Mom, how are you?"

"Oh, fine, fine. The Kleins stopped by for dinner last night." The Kleins do not ensure that my mother is fine; she's just following the scripted pattern of our conversations. It starts with the inquiry of well-being, continues to updates on friends of the family, and concludes with the tricky business of asking about me. This used to be much easier. My parents would telephone every Sunday and Wednesday evening, each on separate phones, and they would hurl questions at me with the enthusiasm of news correspondents. "How's school?" "Did you find matching shoes for your party dress?" "Are you still seeing that boy from your contracts class?" "How was the movie?" Everything, anything, mattered to them. As their only child I was the sun they orbited. The sun's light has faded, I think, looking to my window. The rectangle shows a navy blue world of shadows. The sun is gone.

Today is Monday. The calls do not come as before. Weeks elapse between them, and when I answer the phone there is no overlap of voices, only my mother's. She spends much of the conversation avoiding mention of the pink elephant trumpeting in the middle of the room.

The pink elephant would be my defection to Georgia. When I telephoned with the news of my imminent relocation my father asked, "Georgia, as in the Republic of Georgia by the Black Sea, or Georgia as in the Peach State?" He hoped I meant the former because that Georgia promised unique opportunities to advance the democratic cause of justice. What could Georgia, former land of the Confederacy, offer? My mother worried that there would be no Jews to play or pray with or marry.

"How's Dad?"

"Oh, busy. You know him. Workaholic. I don't think I've seen more than ten minutes of him this week." Her voice, coiled higher and tenser than a tightrope, betrays her. Your father is superbusy so he is not here is her story. My father doesn't want to talk to me is mine.

He carried me on his shoulders and played tea party with me and quizzed me for spelling tests. I brought him papers marked with check pluses and gave him the clay rabbit I made in art class and confided that I didn't like Mom's lasagna but ate it because I didn't want to hurt her feelings. He said he did the same thing.

Now I present my check pluses to my mother. "The DA stopped by my office this morning. Told me what a good job I was doing."

"Honey, that's wonderful." It is, hearing her praise me in her "let's hang your picture on the refrigerator" tone. Is it too much to suppose she will tell my father or that if she does he will care?

"Yeah, it felt good."

"I'm sure he'll write you a glowing recommendation when you decide where to work."

I say nothing. It is clear that, for my parents, until I ascend the Mason-Dixon, no job I possess will be considered real, no house a home, and no existence a life. She may be right.

"Baby?"

"Sorry, Mom, I'm here. I was just spacing out for a moment." Wishing that I could enjoy, not endure, our exchange.

"You're probably tired. Bet you worked late and just got in the door." She has me there. "Just like your father."

Where once there would have been laughter or a mock rueful sigh there is only silence. I am so much like my father that I do not bridge this gap. I make my mother do it.

"Well, princess, I'll let you get back to your life. You take care."

"I will."

"Love you."

"Love you, too. Bye."

I replace the phone and wonder if there is any red wine left. I hope so.

Before I will allow myself food I must change. I twist and bend, hurrying to remove my clothes. The fabrics feel heavy and tight. I exchange the gray suit for a blue tank top and itty-bitty shorts. So short, in fact, they don't deserve the name shorts. They are sho's.

Wine and cheese and crackers for dinner. The wine is Chorey-Les-Beaune "Vieilles Vignes" Dubois, a vintage recommended by Lacey who dated a sommelier from Le Cirque. The cheese is Brie de Meaux, from Anne's Organics on the corner of Third and Cherry. The crackers are Ritz.

I set the plate on the coffee table and my glass atop a coaster. My butt squeaks against the pine boards of the living room floor as I slide forward. One more squeak brings me to the box labeled #11, SMITH COLLEGE. It belongs in the closet where things I cannot bear to part with but do not need are stored. The list cataloguing the box's contents says box #11 holds art, calendars, diploma, papers, photographs, textbooks, and yearbooks. It is the diploma I want.

I dissect the clear packing tape with a scissor blade and fold back the cardboard skin of the box. Before I touch anything inside, I wipe stray cracker crumbs onto my cool thighs. On top, layered in tissue paper, resting on weighty textbooks and copies of political science essays, is the art. Should I bother? Why not? Maybe there is something worthwhile inside to hang on my bare office walls.

The tissue peels away like onionskin. Inside, a dark-eyed girl stares at a book, her eyes too unfocused to be engaged in reading. Her teardrop earrings tangle in her hair. Her charcoal lips curl to the right, an infant smile meant for no one to see. She looks happy, this girl, and I want to reach into the heavy, pitted art paper and wrap my arms about her, kiss her baby-round cheek and promise I won't hurt her ever. But I will. Because the girl is me and before I am done with her she will be thinner and colder and that infant smile will have died a premature death.

Many of the charcoal sketches, pencil drawings, watercolors, and small oil paintings depict me: reading, sitting, sleeping, daydreaming. My friend Katherine painted in school. She often asked me to model for her. Delighted to be selected from a horde of prettier girls, I let her sketch me whenever she wanted. She told me, "You're perfect. Your face shows everything you feel. You're better than twelve different people." She concluded, "You must be a terrible liar." She was right. Back then I could not tell a lie with any confidence. She would marvel at me now.

I set each portrait aside, lingering over a stray curl or a tiny frown line. So young, so vulnerable. I wonder if my colleagues would recognize the girl in these portraits? I set aside the pictures and dig into the box until I find my framed degree, written in Latin, showing that I graduated with a B.A. in political science. I take the diploma and artwork to my bedroom where I lay it atop my queen bed's sheets adorned with huge pink roses. Living here, I felt free to choose a bold romantic floral pattern. Back home I would have restrained myself to a small lilac print or miniature bluebells.

In the living room I reassemble box #11, entombing its contents again. I return it to the box closet and look for box #12 that contains my Harvard Law School diploma. Nudging aside another box, I find box #14, Walters, MacLittle, and Tate. I step back. Oh God, that box. Packed almost a year ago, without the usual care. No list exists for that box. I remember what is stored inside, and what led to its packing.

Most days Henry sat at a forty-five-degree angle, dividing his view between the door and the window. He said he liked to keep an eye on each. He faced the door only when he was entertaining a troubled client. I entered his office on July 8, 1999, to find him seated at his desk. Inside, both senior partners, Walters and MacLittle, stood shoulder to shoulder at the window, staring at the tiny people below them. Both men turned when I said, "I'm sorry. I came to ask—"

Mr. Walters interrupted me with a phlegmatic throat-clearing. This was the second time I had seen him. He rarely visited the offices; his responsibility was maintaining relationships with the upper echelon of clients, those so wealthy that they required someone whose name was on the firm's doors. He had old-man eyebrows: wiry white bushes large enough to nest a small collection of birds. His brows lowered as he focused his pale blue eyes on me.

"Miss Goldberg. We were hoping you might drop by." My hands felt as if they had fallen asleep and were beginning to regain sensation. Prickles of pain danced along my palms.

MacLittle gave me a thorough once-over. His was the stare of a construction worker eyeing a female passerby. That look, coupled with Mr. Walters's inference, worried me. Did they know about Henry and me? I looked at Henry. His face was turned toward the door as if he was expecting someone else, but nobody came.

"Won't you please have a seat?" Mr. Walters said. I sat in the nearest chair. My legs felt as if they were filled with concrete. "I have heard some disturbing news."

Oh, God, I thought. I kept my eyes focused on his wild brows.

"It concerns the Gibbons account."

Gibbons account. Henry had had me work on it several months ago. Work associated with a new venture Gibbons was launching. Travel enterprises.

"Our client is unhappy," Mr. Walters said. His frown indicated he was none too pleased about this. "What we fail to understand is why you chose to establish a separate corporation rather than create a subsidiary corporation." His words were clipped.

"What?" I shook my head.

"Surely you understand that by failing to create a subsidiary considered under tax purposes as a disregarded entity under IRC section 7701, you have exposed Gibbons Inc. to liabilities that may be incurred by Travel Express?" MacLittle asked.

Of course I understood that. I had said as much to Henry, who had been considering creating another corporation, not a subsidiary. I had left my recommendations and paperwork on his desk.

"While we agree it was kind of Henry to give you this extraordinary opportunity to work with such a high-profile client, he agrees it was premature and ill-advised," Walters said.

Premature? Ill-advised? I had been handling this sort of work for six months. I had created more than one subsidiary corporation. Or rather, Henry had. I was not allowed to sign off on the paperwork, not yet. Henry said he would recommend a promotion soon. I was learning so fast.

My hands tingled, hot and cold, hot and cold.

Oh, God. Henry. He had taken the wrong set of papers, those he had given me for review. He had signed off on the wrong set, not mine. Mine were flawless.

"I didn't—" I began.

MacLittle interrupted. "Shhh," he said. He put his finger to his lips, a parody of a librarian.

"We understand you must be upset. It isn't every day you have such an opportunity."

I broke my gaze from MacLittle long enough to look at Henry. He watched us as if we were actors. His hands rested limp in his lap; his shoulders sagged. He was not going to contradict them. I looked away.

"I am afraid, however, that we are going to have to reduce your workload in consideration of this development."

"Your SEC filing work looks very thorough," he said, nodding.

No. Not SEC filings. It was elevated paralegal work.

I leaned back into my chair as he approached to stand beside Mr. Walters. The two loomed over me like disapproving parents. "You will want to pass off any other open casework you have to other associates. Some new filing work has been settled on your desk this afternoon." They were demoting me for a mistake for which I was not responsible.

A bird flew past the window, a small, dirty pigeon. "Rats with wings," people called them. There were worse kinds of rats.

My mind raced. Even if I managed to survive the demotion, what then? Work my way back to a position I held now? What if somebody made another mistake? Would I be fired? Blame the new, Jew girl? Why not?

I flexed my hands. Why not?

"That's kind of you," I said. I coughed, trying to clear my throat.

"But unnecessary. In fact, it's fortuitous that you are both present." My hands felt as if they were on fire. What was I doing?

Walters cocked his head to the side and MacLittle frowned. They did not know what to make of this.

"I have been offered another job, which I intend to accept." The words came out faster than I intended. Bluffing was never my strength.

"Well, well," MacLittle said.

"Where?" Henry finally spoke. He stared at me, his eyes dark. With regret?

"Georgia."

"Georgia?" he repeated.

"Well, well." MacLittle seemed not to know what to say. Good.

"The district attorney is looking for a new prosecuting attorney," I said.

"Criminal law?" Walters sounded scandalized. Never mind that his clients evaded the law sixteen ways to Sunday.

I nodded. "You may consider this my notice." I stood. My legs trembled. "I was going to offer you two weeks, but since you've reassigned my casework it looks as though I'll have time for a long lunch this afternoon. I'll sign my termination agreement today."

As I left the room I could hear them talking over each other. It had not gone at all as they had planned, but then, it had not gone as I had expected, either. I had been accused of ineptitude for which my lover was guilty, not me. And now, oh God. Now I had to make the job I had thrown at them mine. The job I had read about online earlier that morning.

Why *that* job?

Because when I read the pay description and the location, I thought, "Who in their right mind would take this?" Thus, it was the first and only job I remembered when Walters and MacLittle were playing bad cop, worse cop. That job, public prosecutor, had the bonus of showing contempt for their culture of greed and lies. It was perfect. The worst thing I could tell them.

Contrary to my claim, it took me two days to leave. I had to sign many forms, in triplicate, that severed my connection to Walters, MacLittle, and Tate. I handed off unfinished business to other associates, some smug-faced and superior, aware of my disgrace, others worried, as if they too could be exiled to the South if they screwed up. It was a quiet exit. No one threw me a farewell party. I packed my Metropolitan Museum of Art calendar, my framed photographs, law books, and the pot that held the long-ago-extinct plant I bought my first day. I carried the box out of the office on July 10, 1999. The box that is now #14.

I close the door on the closet and all it contains and retreat to my bedroom where I move the diploma and artwork to my desktop. These things are not safe on my bed. They could fall victim to my restless arms, which reach out and search for things that elude me in dreams, running too fast for me to catch.

Chapter Seven

July 3, 2000

This must stop, this dizzying déjà vu. Perhaps I could begin varying my routine, or perhaps Carl could stop calling my home telephone number every morning. Can't he wait the twelve minutes it will take for me to get to the office? Why does he need to track my caseloads?

I set down the iron and examine my skirt. Wrinkle free. I wriggle into the still-hot fabric, twisting in a parody of dance. When did I last dance? My feet slide into the baby-powder-sprinkled interior of my black leather heels. Maddie's wedding, five months ago. I danced to old favorites with the girls until my feet hurt and then I took off my shoes and danced some more. Lacey threatened to hire a lawyer if I stepped on her feet one more time. She claimed she would seek emotional damages as well as physical. Why emotional? "Because it causes me great distress to know my best friend can't dance for shit," she told me.

Semidrunk and stomping to a beat unheard by any other person, I smiled and said, "You're my best friend, too."

My blue and white kitchen clock shows the little hand at seven, the big hand at two. I'll be at work by seven-thirty. My routine used to deliver me to my office a half hour to an hour early. No wonder Carl worries.

Today his call informed me that I have been appointed cocounsel in Ben's case against Calvin Washington, a man accused of two murders. Ben and I have never partnered on a case. If Jeffrey Barr had not quit, if Ben had not been ill recently, and if Carl were not scheduled to go to Bermuda soon, it would not have happened. I imagine Ben's reaction to the news of our impending teamwork. He probably bellowed, "Goldberg Junior? I'm babysitting Goldberg Junior? The kid is barely out of diapers."

Legally speaking, he has a point. I have been practicing criminal law for six months. This case will be my first murder trial. Until now aggravated assault, arson, armed robbery, and involuntary manslaughter have composed my trial experiences. After several fumbles and one explicit curse I wrench the childproof cap off a bottle of antacids and chew three tablets. They leave chalky residue on my teeth. I will have to brush again when I reach the office.

Coffee consumed, teeth clean, and e-mail reviewed and prioritized at eight-thirty A.M. By ten o'clock I have rid my desk of paperwork related to two closed cases and scheduled two meetings with defense attorneys hoping to find me in a lenient mood.

Ben steps inside my office at ten thirty-five. His wide body manages to fill every crevice of space. "Hello, Natalie," he says. I lean back in my chair.

"Good morning, Ben."

"You have heard you will be assisting me on the Washington case?"

"Yes. Cocounsel." I do not care for his word choice. Assisting, as if I'm a first-year intern. "I look forward to it."

He rubs his beardless chin and rests his substantial weight on his back foot. He looks at me as though he is in the market for a house and I am a real fixer-upper. I allow myself the luxury of crossing my stiff legs, which draws his gaze down in Pavlovian predictability.

Ben removes his reading glasses from his dress shirt pocket and begins wiping at them with a handkerchief the size of a small tablecloth. "This is your first murder trial?" He knows it is.

"I remember my first murder trial." He stops rubbing his glasses and shifts his gaze to the bookcase, but he is not looking at the *Georgia Code* books; he is looking through them. "*People* v. *Drummond.* Man stabbed his wife and three children to death. Claimed the devil made him do it." His low chuckle indicates what he thought of the defense then and now. "So I sent him to meet the fellow giving the orders."

His brown eyes return to me. "He went to the electric chair in '92." His smile is wistful, as if remembering a love affair. "We'll be seeking the death penalty."

Before I can protest or ask a question he adds, "We'll meet today at three o'clock. My office." He is gone before I can recover.

The death penalty. My fingers trace the wood grain of Guvnor's desk. In junior high debate club I chose "con" in the debate on the death penalty. In college I marched on the Capitol with the National Coalition to Abolish the Death Penalty. I volunteered with Amnesty International while in New York, working to convince states to impose moratoriums on capital punishment sentences. I am one of the 30 percent of Americans who think that killing convicted felons is not the answer.

When I took this job I knew I might find myself in this position. The 1973 Supreme Court decided in *Furman* v. *Georgia* to establish a moratorium on death penalty sentences on the grounds that they constituted cruel and unusual punishment. They were resurrected a mere four years later in *Gregg* v. *Georgia*. Notice the common name in these cases?

When I accepted this position I swore to uphold the Constitution of the State of Georgia. The decision to sentence a convict to death is made by the jury and must be upheld by the judge. The decision to seek the death penalty is made by the prosecutor. It's Ben's call. This time I forgo the antacids and reach for the aspirin.

Carl visits my office at eleven-thirty. He was "just in the area." His language implies he never intended to arrive anywhere or speak to anyone in his entire life; connections are happy accidents to Carl.

He stalks the perimeter of my office. He does not take note of my stare. He is too busy pacing, looking for objects of interest that are not there.

"Can I help you, Carl?" I do not want to help anyone right now, but I want him to stop pacing. He is making me swimmy-headed, the local term for "dizzy."

"You know about securities, right?" He halts his long-legged stride and turns his torso in a quick pivot that speaks of hours spent on basketball courts. My admiration for his physical grace is tempered by concern for his expression. Carl's ever-present apprehension manifests itself in tics like pencil tapping, not in his appearance. He always looks put together, assured. Now, however, his face is twisted with worry, causing lines to appear about his forehead, eyes, and mouth. His blue eyes are foggy.

"I know about securities as they pertain to corporations."

His head bobs as if a puppeteer is pulling it from above. He walks to my desk and sits in a chair without asking. Oh, dear. This means trouble. Carl never takes a seat in my office without asking first. His momma wouldn't abide such manners.

"Why do you want to know about securities?" Carl handles

the sexual assault cases. How would a case of his relate to securities law?

He leans toward me, head poking forward and down, turtlelike. I look to my open door and watch a paralegal pass by carrying two reams of copy paper. Her gaze lingers on Carl. Nothing new there, all the paralegals adore Carl. He is attractive, single, and, most important, he treats them well. I rise and close the door. I suspect whatever he is about to unburden deserves a closed door.

"It's my sister," he begins, and the slow lingering of the word "sist-uh" is more than Southern; it is love and despair in two syllables. His fingers wrestle each other as he tells me about Sarah, his younger sister. She is twenty-eight and married, with two kids, Billy and Lily, ages six and four. Her husband, William, works as a financial consultant at Hall Investments. A vein swells near Carl's temple and throbs purple against his hairline.

"William beats Sarah." He lifts his head to stare at me.

He does not think William has abused the children, not yet, but Sarah has visited the emergency room several times with stories of household accidents. He has tried to convince her to leave William, to take the children and go. She will not. His head sinks under the weight of this burden.

"Have the police been called?" Sometimes neighbors alert the police. Too many times they do not, believing that what happens next door is none of their business.

Carl says it has happened twice but the cops have been persuaded that the domestic misunderstanding was just that. His Macon police contacts are of little help. His sister lives in Savannah.

"Why do you want to know about securities?" I ask.

"William is a snake." I sense Carl has substituted "snake" for a word he deems unfit for my ladylike ears. "I think he is involved in illegal transactions, fraud. I have suspected it for some time, but I don't know much about that area." He shrugs. "If I could find evidence that he has been abusing his clients' accounts, charges could be brought against him."

White-collar crime. I shake my head. Even if Carl's brother-in-law were convicted, the chances that he would serve time are slim. Plus, he could be forced to forfeit assets, which could hurt Sarah and the children financially.

"It's tough to prove fraud, especially on an individual level." This won't work. It's too complex. I bounce my right shoe off and on my heel, off and on. Didn't Deidre Kendall from Smith start a domestic abuse agency? Somewhere in Charleston? I wonder if she is listed on the alumnae pages?

"Natalie?"

My shoe drops mid-bounce. I bend forward to retrieve and replace it. "Sorry, I was thinking."

"I could tell."

"I want to help," I say, using my best Mrs. Graszcow voice. Mrs. Graszcow was my second-grade teacher and the queen of lecturers, stern but kind. "But I don't think this is the best way. Even if we could prove fraud and he were convicted and sent away, the process would take well over a year. And it's very unlikely." He looks at me as if I have trampled his sand castle.

"I know some people involved with domestic abuse, in centers and agencies. I could talk to them. See what they think. And maybe I could meet her, your sister Sarah." It's not much, but it's all I have, and if I had more to offer it still might not be enough.

My mother volunteered at a shelter for domestic abuse victims when I was too small to understand why the women who slept in bunk beds, like at camp, were not overjoyed by the arrangements. I played with children whose toys bore the marks of tough love: dolls with severed limbs and stuffed animals with stains on their yellow and blue fur. I think of those women, some of whom returned to their homes after a week at the shelter, too scared by the prospect of starting over to stay.

"She might not leave him," I want to say, but I don't because I suspect he knows. Instead I make a note to track down Deidre and contact her. My gaze slides over my calendar. July 3, the day before Independence Day, a day to celebrate basic freedoms like life, liberty, and the right to not serve as someone's punching bag.

Carl asks to borrow a pen. This show of etiquette reassures me. He notes his sister's name and address in a cramped, masculine print and tells me that she stays at home with the children while William works. "Thanks, Nat, I mean Natalie." His tanned cheeks flush.

"You can call me Nat." He rises from his chair. "Everyone does." Now it's my turn to blush, because no one here refers to me as anything but Natalie or Miss Goldberg. "I mean, my friends and family do."

He nods, fingers tapping his thighs, anxiety restored. "You won't mention this to anyone?" he asks, hand on the doorknob. "I mean—"

"No, I won't say anything," I promise. Don't worry, Carl. I can keep a secret.

In law school they don't teach you about keeping secrets. They speak of client confidentiality, yes. And they talk of ethics, of morals, and of justice, never explaining that these concepts might be, by their nature, incompatible. Defense attorneys adopt a "don't ask, don't tell" policy regarding their client's guilt. Prosecutors bargain with lesser criminals in attempts to catch bigger criminals. Police present evidence gained using questionable methods and procedures.

During the first criminal case I assisted on I spoke with a policeman who had discovered the bloodstained hammer used in an assault. He said the hammer was found beside the suspect's back porch. The defendant claimed the hammer was locked in a closet inside the house and that the house was searched after my policeman kicked the door in.

I can now recognize a "TGTBT" story, too good to be true, in the first telling. Each such story recalls my father, who used to rant against policemen beating confessions from suspects, of violating their Miranda rights, of planting evidence. All violations of justice.

That hammer I mentioned? It was used on the legs and arms of a fifteen-year-old who will always walk with a limp.

This work has shown me why cops with nicotine-stained hands sometimes overstep boundaries. They want to see the guilty sent away, to keep the rest of us safe, and they suspect playing by the rules won't get it done. I'm still sent running for a bottle of Maalox when presented with a TGTBT story, but I am learning not to ask questions when I sense the answers will not prove useful and lead to nights of interrupted sleep.

I stop drawing circles on the paper before me. The tiny doodles are symptomatic of excitement. I open a new notebook and begin making a to-do list for Carl's sister. My pen forms neat words, coherent thoughts. Inside, however, my mind chugs like a roller coaster with too much fuel and no off switch. This is what I love: helping people and solving puzzles. It's what I always wanted to do.

Someone has installed a revolving door outside my office. This would explain why foot traffic has tripled today. First Ben, then Carl, Will's secretary Janice, Phil from Victim's Aid, and Trudy, a temp who wanted the telephone number for the Georgia Bureau of Investigation. Why she asked me I don't know. Maybe because I'm not the sort to send someone away. Yet how did she know?

When I arrived here I did not cultivate friends. I replied to any and all personal questions with monosyllabic answers, offering nothing more than was polite. Perhaps the ice has thawed. Perhaps

I'm not quite the bitch I was, if people are approaching me with personal matters. Even Officer Wilkins's teasing the other day had a friendly banter to it, like kindergarten boys who pull your hair. A glance at my watch shows I have seven minutes to collect my thoughts and get to Ben's office. My goodwill shatters into crystal shards of annoyance.

I am prepared to reprise my role of bitch for Ben.

Chapter Eight

I had planned to drive to one of my three standard restaurants for takeout, but instead I detour to Bruster's Old Fashioned Ice Cream and Yogurt. A line of people extends from the pink Formica counter to the door with the tinkling bell. By the time I reach the front I have read every flavor available four times. The list does not influence me to try anything new. I order a half-gallon of pink lemonade sherbet and watch the high school girl behind the counter scoop and smoosh the pale ice cream into the cardboard container. I settle the tub in the deep hollow of my passenger seat and hope it doesn't melt into a pink puddle on the way home.

The ice cream and I make it without melting, though it's a near thing. The evening air's humidity makes breathing aerobic exercise. I huff and puff my way indoors where I stow the ice cream in the freezer and change into my play clothes. I touch my sneaker toes three times, then reach to the sky, my version of exercise. Then I grab my keys and the ice cream and head next door to visit Mrs. Dayton, my neighbor and gardening mentor.

Halfway there I remember to look for a rock. I squat low to the ground and crab-walk along, stopping every few feet to pick up one. Nope, too small. No, too ordinary. Near the end of the drive I spot one. Pink quartz, if memory of high school geology serves me. I put it in my shorts pocket and hurry because the ice cream container has begun to sweat.

I wait atop the house's side steps, the front door being for company and salesmen, not regulars such as myself. Two knocks are all it takes to summon Mrs. Dayton, known to everyone as Lala. Her real name is Evelyn, and even she cannot remember how the nickname took. Something about a younger cousin with a lisp, she thinks.

Lala's wrinkles smooth as a grin pulls her tanned face taut. "Natalie! Come in, come in." She waves one arm in circles, like an airstrip worker signaling a plane. "I was thinking of you this afternoon." I follow her through the photograph-lined entryway to the kitchen where she takes the ice cream from me. "Pink lemonade. My favorite. Of course, you can only get it in the summer. I suppose if they had it year round it wouldn't be as special." She sounds unconvinced.

"I suppose we will never know," I reply with mock gravity.

Lala smiles as she gathers two cherry-printed bowls and two spoons. "I shouldn't eat so many sweets," she says, wrestling the top off the ice cream. "Duke is going to burn my ears when I see him." Duke was her husband who died three years ago, killed in a car accident on Emery Highway. Lala often speculates about how he will react to her behavior when he sees her in heaven.

She hands me a bowl, and I have to smother a laugh because she took the bowl with the most sherbet. I pass through the dining room whose prevailing decorating theme is doilies. Lala likes lace, and hand-tatted all the dining room doilies herself. I had no idea that the word for making doilies was "tat" until she told me. She said it often appears in crossword puzzles. Lala can complete the *New York Times* Saturday crossword puzzle without cheating.

Stepping down Lala's back stairs is like leaving earth for heaven. The backyard has small footpaths running through tall stalks of colorful, sweet-smelling flowers. We walk to the middle of the garden, where seating exists in the form of a bench and three Adirondack chairs. The seats are gathered around a small pond filled with large goldfish. Surrounding the pool are piles of stones donated by Lala's friends, a mosaic of memories. Some have traveled from as far away as Thailand. I rest my bowl on the arm of the chair before fishing the quartz from my pocket.

"Lovely! Where's it from?" she asks as she settles it atop the other rocks. For now, my quartz is King of the Hill.

I often pick up rocks around town. I once asked Lacey to send me a rock from Central Park. She mailed a bright blue pebble along with a note that said: *I understand you miss the city, but a rock from the park? Why not something more fitting, like a used condom or syringe?*

I tell Lala it came from my driveway.

"Perfect! The scene of our first meeting."

She is correct. Two days after my arrival in Macon I exited my car to find a woman in a tangerine sundress with a blue-rinsed perm standing at the edge of my driveway, clutching a bouquet of flowers. I looked at her tanned, age-spotted face and thought, "Not another Jehovah's Witness!" I had suffered a visit from an elderly pair of proselytizers the prior morning.

Lala told me that her first thought upon seeing me was, That girl looks like she hasn't seen the sun all summer. Better get her to the garden. I allowed her to walk me there, expecting her to preach about my eternal soul at any moment.

Lilies, hyacinths, asters, lilacs, myrtle, daisies, honeysuckle, sunflowers, roses, gardenias, all bloom in Lala's sanctuary. I wonder if the fish swimming lazy circles realize how lucky they are to be surrounded by such beauty. Then I wonder if fish can smell or see color, and if they can't, are these fish any happier than fish imprisoned in pet store tanks?

It's all about perspective. This oasis Lala has created feels special because it is unlike every other part of my life. I wish my mother, who loves gardening, would meet Lala and visit her garden, but that would involve coming here and acknowledging that my job is more than a temporary position. It would demand that my parents treat my decision to come to Macon as something other than a descent into temporary insanity.

Too bad. Mom would like Lala, admire her tenacity. Lala carries twenty-pound bags of mulch in arms vivid with green-blue veins. She winces after a full day of bending to plant, weed, water, and prune, but shoos away the idea of a helper. "They would pull up all of the weeds," she said when I suggested she hire someone.

"But you pull up weeds," I pointed out, knowing she did, because I had seen her pulling the gosh-darned weeds choking her daisies and heard her scolding them.

"Not all the weeds. I keep the ones I like." I should have known that the woman who captures insects in her house and carries them to safety outdoors (except those harmful to her garden) spares the lives of her favorite weeds.

Under Lala's tutelage I have learned more than I suspected there was to know about flora. My mother, who tried to interest me in gardening, would not recognize the child who said flowers were boring in the woman kneeling in the dirt digging around visible worms. This was another childhood objection I had to gardening: "It's messy." I sigh, wishing messy was an area confined to dirt. Messy applies to so many areas of my life, including my job.

I had known my three o'clock meeting with Ben wouldn't go

well. It might have helped if I had not begun by asking, "Why capital punishment?" Ben spoke for five minutes about public safety, the victim's family's sense of closure, and recidivism.

I breathed in and out of my nose, refusing to get involved in a debate. "What I meant was why are we seeking the death penalty on *this* case?"

"Calvin Washington committed felonious murder. The aggravating circumstances involved compel us to seek the strictest justice." His sonorous delivery raised suspicions that he was auditioning a piece of his opening speech for me.

"What aggravating circumstances are you citing?"

Ben rocked in his chair, a motion made easier by his excess thirty pounds. A smile separated his lips to reveal a mouth full of teeth that could benefit from a bleaching or two. "Why, Natalie, you don't mean to tell me you are not familiar with Title 42, Chapter 5, Section 85 of the Georgia Code detailing aggravating circumstances?"

"I am."

"Then you should have no trouble listing them." The smile grew wider. I glared at his lips. He could not be serious. "I realize you're still new to our humble state but it might be nice if you learned the laws."

That did it. I recited all ten aggravating circumstances in a flat monotone that implied I could have gone on to recite the Georgia Code in its entirety if I felt so inclined.

"Once you have reviewed the files I am sure you will have no trouble identifying which factors we will be citing." He slid a file box marked "J. Barr-Washington" to the edge of his desk, just out of arm's reach. He wasn't going to give me an inch, on anything. The reminder of Jeffrey's defection made me wonder if working with Ben was what drove him away.

I have escaped too, for now, to a place without tension. Shifting my legs, I sigh. I envy Lala's fish their simple lives.

"Sounds like you've had yourself a day," she observes. I squirm, aware that I have not said two words since we came out here. Some guest I am.

"I'm sorry, Lala. It has been quite a day."

She chuckles. "You know what would make you feel better?" I look down at my empty sherbet bowl, amazed. I was not aware that I had been lifting the spoon to my mouth. Her chuckle deepens. "Not more sherbet. Planting. I've got some impatiens I need to put in this evening. I was waiting for the ground to cool."

I rise from my chair, anxious to help. Lala is in good health, but I worry that she might overexert herself. Planting the flowers, however, turns out to require little effort. We dig small holes in the soil, settle the impatiens into their new homes, and sprinkle them with water. Lala sings a medley of Frank Sinatra tunes. She claims the flowers dig Sinatra. I hum along, unsure of the words.

There is dirt on my knees, on my hands, and, according to Lala, on my face, but I don't care. I rest my butt on the heels of my sneakers and sigh, a happy sigh this time. "Will these bloom every year?" I am slow to learn perennials and annuals.

"Nope." She rinses her spade with a stream of water from the watering can and replaces it in its appointed garden toolbox slot. "These will stay around until October or so and then *pfft*!" She taps the earth around the base of one of the new flowers.

"That's not very long."

"Some flowers do not last long, but it makes their time in the garden that much more special, in a way. Nothing lasts forever." I wonder if she is thinking of her husband.

"Do you suppose they go to flower heaven?" I might as well have asked if she believed in fairies.

She doesn't laugh. She places the watering can beside the tools. "Flowers decompose and become part of the earth and in turn fertilize other flowers. That's a sort of afterlife. The same for trees and bugs and animals. Duke would accuse me of blasphemy for saying so, but I'm not sure a body needs any other kind of heaven. Giving life to a rose isn't so bad. A person could do worse." She stares about her, at the vivid colors made brighter by the settling darkness.

I squeeze her spotted hands twice. She stands near my own five feet and three inches, the years pulling her closer to the earth, an irresistible magnet. "Thank you," I say.

"Anytime, Natalie."

I leave by the gate. Looking at the purple blossoms beside the white wood fence I think of Lala's afterlife. It would appear her heaven allows nonbelievers inside. Not a bad deal for those lacking faith, or those who have mislaid it. Images of Temple Beth Shalom return to me: the lions flanking the two stone tablets above the Holy Ark, the siddur's thin, fragrant pages, rows of male heads covered by small black discs.

How long has it been since I have been to temple? Years. Would I be able to follow the service if I returned? Would I feel capable of declaring God's Holiness with the congregation during the Kedushah? Or would I have to admit that my conversations with God, like those with my parents, have become infrequent and painful?

Just in case, I think, touching the mezuzah hanging outside the doorframe of my back door. I kiss the fingers that touched it. Just in case.

Chapter Nine

July 13, 2000

I can't be wrong on this. Please, God, do not let me be wrong on this. Ten minutes ago I challenged Ben on a point of law regarding Georgia's "seven deadly sins" parole legislation. His phone rang as we argued. He said he had to take the call. I have jogged to my office to check. If I am wrong it's crow pie for a week. Who am I kidding? My diet will be crow, crow, crow for life, life, life.

My fingers speed-type on my keyboard, fueled by adrenaline and fear. "Please be right," I whisper under my breath, over and over, turning it into a chant. I process the query and wait for the results. Aha! It was established January 1, 1995. I knew it! A constitutional amendment effective January 1,1995, all but abolished parole for Georgia's seven most violent crimes known as the "deadly sins." Murder, rape, kidnapping, armed robbery, aggravated sodomy, aggravated sexual battery, and aggravated child molestation. Each carries a minimum sentence of ten years without parole. I knew it was 1995, not 1994. A loud splatter of rain draws me to the window. I smile. The rain may be falling with monsoon intensity outside my window, but in my office it is a sunshine day.

Ben has been nipping at me all week, questioning my knowledge of law, of jury selection, of lunch choices. He dislikes sushi. Worse is that I have found him better versed on the first two. Ben scorns the concept of professional jury consultants, who recommend which jurors to keep and which to dismiss during voir dire, but he is familiar with their tactics and has read the latest literature pertaining to their work. I assumed he dismissed all things on personal bias. It appears he does not, though he did tell me he wouldn't eat raw fish prepared by Japs if the president of the U.S. asked him to. Good old Ben. I didn't point out that his belly might benefit from more California rolls and fewer cheeseburgers.

I shuffle my way back to his office, doing a half-dance of glee. Will, passing by, brown-green eyes ringed with circles, blinks twice and says, "Natalie?" I smile but don't break stride. "Are you doing the Hustle?" he asks, causing heads to pop out of cubicles like jack-in-the-boxes. All eyes are on me.

"No way," I shout. "The Electric Slide." My grin does not waver as I shuffle the remainder of the way to Ben's door. My knock is perfunctory. I have half my torso inside his office when I see he is not alone. I'm stuck. A petite blonde sits opposite Ben, her hands clenching his. Her nails are lacquered cotton-candy pink and she wears two rings: one small gold band on her left ring finger and a sapphire ring on her right middle finger. She cocks her head toward me, and the motion, combined with her small dark eyes, reminds me of a sparrow. She has the bone structure: thin, little, easy to break. I retreat with a quick "I'm sorry" and head for the ladies' room.

The doors hang open on all three stalls. No one is primping before the mirror or washing their hands. It's just me. Should I return to my office and wait for Ben to find me? Or should I check to see if the blonde is gone? Under yellow-green lights that make me look jaundiced, I rub at a small speck of mascara that has migrated south, below my lower lashes. I wonder who she is. The way her hands gripped his, as if holding on to a life preserver. His wife? I wag my head at the mirror girl. Just because she seemed intimate doesn't mean she is his wife. You ought to know that, I reprimand myself.

The other woman, that's what I was, for twenty months, Henry Tate's mistress. I worked with him for five months on the case that introduced us. During tutorials on structured transactions and manipulating financial statements I received, gratis, lessons on desire. Hiding my longing from Henry became a task more difficult than reconciling multiple Forms 3, 4, and 5 for our biggest clients. In the end, my efforts failed. My too obvious face, the one Katherine liked to draw, gave me away. A week after the SEC investigation of our client ended, Henry invited me to the Michelangelo Hotel's lobby for drinks. When I saw he sat alone on a red-patterned sofa, sipping Scotch, I tried to act surprised. When he handed me my martini his long fingers caressed mine. I stared at the etched lines of his knuckles, the dark hairs on the back of his hand, so fine they were almost invisible.

He had the room card in his wallet. I followed him into a red and brass elevator and down a hallway with carpet so thick our feet made no sound as we walked. Inside the room I stared at the buttons on Henry's blue shirt, unable to look at his face, not ready. When his fingers crept into the hairs at the bottom of my scalp, massaging, I knew he saw it all: the desire, the guilt, the fear, the hope, the joy. The brush of coolness against my scalp, the hard metal of Henry's wedding band, did not jolt me from my sexual dream. I arched up and back and he whispered my name and Natalie was no longer a singsong of syllables used to summon me to the kitchen table. I was reborn, bathed in Henry's kisses and given a new name, a long-drawn-out sigh. *Nat-ah-leeee.*

Standing before him, dizzy with sex and power, I forgot that I had ever worn pigtails or braces or training bras. I felt as if I had been born full woman, Athena from Zeus's brow, with heavy breasts and dark pubic hair as curly as that atop my head. I focused on the serpent of feeling rearranging itself within me, twining closer to my damp vagina. When Henry stripped me bare of all my clothes, of the lace panties I wore because I planned for every eventuality, I lay atop the semicool sheets and brought him to me and in me with my right hand, the same hand I used to write with, to carry heavy bags and to masturbate with. And then he knew everything, everything no one else knew. I screamed. It hurt, and even as my flesh resisted, I thought this is how it should be. It shouldn't be easy.

Adultery. In one moment, I broke multiple Commandments. But that first morning, lying within the cave of Henry's chest, I did not wonder if his wife was worried, or if he told her he was away on business. I marveled that the rhythmic drumming of his heart could dance against my spine. The woman he had pledged his devotion to was somewhere else and I kept her away from my mind as long as I could. It was not as hard as it should have been.

I met Henry's wife once, at the firm's holiday party, held at Windows on the World, atop the World Trade Center. I had not begun working with Henry yet. I spent much of the party staring out the windows, looking at the Statue of Liberty, remote atop her pedestal. During one of these moments, a respite from discussions of plans with coworkers about the holidays, a voice said, "Is it time to go yet?" Without turning I knew the speaker was female and beautiful. You could hear it in her voice, the expectation of agreement.

She was lovely. Fine boned, her pale hair swept up in a loose chignon, the kind that could never hold my wild hair. She wore a long black dress and a bright diamond choker. I smiled at her apparent disdain for the party while considering whether she ever ate dessert. Her shoulders looked as sharp as her cheekbones.

"This thing seems to get worse each year." She swallowed a mouthful of champagne to emphasize her point.

"I'm sorry. Do you work for the firm?" I couldn't believe I would have missed another female lawyer, especially one this attractive.

"Lord, no. My husband, Henry, does. He's over there." She gestured with her drinking hand, a quick movement. I had no hope of identifying her husband from the crowd of suited half-drunk men.

"It's a nice view," I offered, casting a pitying glace at Lady Liberty, forgotten and unloved.

The woman stared out the wall of windows, but I sensed she saw nothing but her own reflection. "I hate heights," she said, and then, as "We Wish You a Merry Christmas" began sounding from the band, "and I loathe Christmas carols."

"I like them," I confessed before adding, "I'm Jewish" as if that excused me.

"Huh." She took another long swallow of champagne. "I'm Hilary."

"Natalie." Inspired by the song, I told her, "It means born on Christmas. My name."

"How funny." Her face tightened with thought. "Did your parents know?"

"I'm sure. They named me after my grandmother."

I don't think she heard me. She glared at the band as they segued into "Winter Wonderland."

"I think it's high time to leave." She set her empty glass on the table beside us. "It was nice meeting you."

"Nice meeting you, too," I replied, though she was several feet away by then.

I recognized the woman in Henry's silver-framed photograph atop his desk. Hilary, the beauty from the holiday party. It made his desire for me more amazing. That he possessed her and wanted me. Funny little me with my dimpled elbows and wild hair. To think I was better than her made me rich with power, heady with lust. It also made me sick with guilt, at first, but I developed a tolerance over time.

My patience, however, still needs work, as seen by my current situation. I extend and contort my neck to peer through the small slit of Ben's open door. He looks up and sees me. "Are you going to spy on me all day?"

"I wasn't spying." I am appalled by how much I sound like a sullen six-year-old. "I did not want to interrupt you and your . . . visitor."

"My wife, Jenny." Ben seems amused by my discomfort.

"Oh. She's very pretty." I can't think of anything else to say.

"I think so. Now about the physical evidence. I have scheduled a meeting with officers Wilkins and Cox. They handled the case. We'll call Cox to testify."

"Why not Wilkins?"

"Because Cox is older."

"Yes, and Wilkins is blacker." Ben doesn't argue this. Cox is white. I tell him, "If we are going death penalty on this you don't want a suggestion of racism. The defendant is black. So were the victims. Introduce the white cop and the white lawyers and, hell, why not an all-white jury, and you have yourself a problem. If we win the conviction, there may be an appeal. Better to have no suggestion of—"

Ben interrupts, "Defense has been trying to play the race card. During the appeals hearing, Landry argued that the state flag symbolized the history of racism and that its presence in the court would influence jurors." Ben's voice leaves little doubt how he felt about this argument. I don't say anything about the Confederate battle flag that dominates the state flag and how uncomfortable it makes me. There has been talk of changing it, but it's amounted to nothing more than that.

"I think he may have been using the flag as a decoy." His voice grows warmer. "He pushed to have Washington appear in civilian clothes, arguing that the jumpsuit and shackles reinforced a false presumption of guilt."

"What happened?" I was not present for the unified appeal hearing. Ben had handled it, and Jeffrey aided him. That was in mid-May, while I toiled to convict robbers and drunk drivers, not murderers.

The unified appeal hearing marks a sea change in our legal system. Death row inmates once possessed many chances to reverse their sentence, complicating and lengthening the appeals process. Georgia adopted a unified appeal system that gathers all the issues on which a defendant can appeal into one document. This document can be brought to the state and federal appellate courts only once. Ben is implying that Landry, lead defense counsel, brought a laundry list. With a client facing death, one could hardly expect him to do otherwise.

"Washington can wear a suit, but he will be shackled. The judges pointed out that Washington was accused of two murders and shouldn't be allowed to blend in with other civilians." Score one for us.

After a moment Ben says, "We will get Wilkins to testify."

My euphoria is severed by anxiety. I hope Wilkins does not discover I am the reason he is testifying. He won't thank me for the honor.

"You sure are going great guns at this for someone who professes to hate the death penalty." He stares at me as if he expects me to come clean and confess that I'm only masquerading as a lefty liberal.

"I don't endorse a terminal punishment in a system of justice that is flawed. Mistakes get made. Wrongful convictions do happen. But my issues with the death penalty are just that, my issues. I am not going to jeopardize this case because of its possible outcome. I would not do that." I direct a steady gunslinger stare at him while I talk.

He issues a loud "humph." "We're meeting with Wilkins and Cox tomorrow at eleven."

"I have an arraignment at eleven." Why does it never occur to him to check with me before he schedules meetings?

He glares at me through his thick glasses. "I'll see if they can push it back. Would one o'clock be possible?"

"S'art eich?" Oh, man, he has driven me to mumbling in Yiddish.

"What?"

"Anytime after noon will be fine." Asshole.

"Fine. I will let you know when the meeting is scheduled. Until then, you have the files? Review the crime-scene report before we meet." As if I need him to explain how to prep for a meeting.

I am halfway out of Ben's door when I pause to say, "Oh, Ben?"

"Yes?" He slaps the papers he was reading onto his desk.

"The seven deadly sins legislature was enacted on January 1, 1995, meaning that the first class of graduates will be released in 2005, not 2004. Just thought you would want to know. Best to keep current on these things."

I leave with the last word still vibrating on my lips, tasting sweeter than sugar.

Chapter Ten

Blood appears shiny and black in photographs when still fresh, so I know Marcus Rhodes was not dead long when the crime scene photographer took these snapshots. A puddle of black pools about his beaten face, a pulpy, bruised thing, a third missing where two bullets tore through it. Marcus's long body is twisted, hands underneath his back where Calvin Washington tied them before he beat Marcus. The two nine-millimeter bullets killed him, not the baseball bat. *The murder was outrageously or wantonly vile, horrible, or inhuman in that it involved torture, depravity of mind, or an aggravated battery to the victim.* Okay, Ben, I assume we will be citing this along with *The murder was committed while the offender was engaged in the commission of another capital felony, aggravated battery, burglary, or arson in the first degree.* It doesn't get much more aggravated than battery by bat.

I forgive myself for waiting to look at these photographs. Though I should have reviewed them sooner, I knew the stark images would settle like silt to the bottom of my mind, ready to be stirred again to the surface by another future case. I exhale through my nose, a breathing trick that is supposed to center me by making me concentrate on my own breath. All it does is make me more aware that the people before me cannot breathe. I breathe through my mouth and lift the last photograph of Marcus.

In this photo there is less shiny black liquid pooled about the corpse, and no signs of beating, but there is a hole in the small chest that should not be there. Dominic Brown, a student at Burke Elementary School. The school where Marcus Rhodes worked as a janitor, where Calvin Washington hunted him down. Calvin threatened to kill Marcus days earlier because Marcus had ridiculed Calvin's favorite sports team, the Washington Redskins. Why did he kill little Dominic? Our best guess is he interrupted Calvin's vengeance.

I squint at the photo. Small black boy, lying dead. Familiar somehow. From the news? No. When Ben first talked of the case I realized it came in while I was out sick with the office flu. The small outcry that accompanied these murders, the rush to arraign the murderer, all had happened while I lay sniffling in bed, my arms too heavy and achy to move more than a few inches.

I lift the photo and regard the second. "I don't know why she swallowed the fly." The song is in my head before I realize, before clarity drops my mouth open. Dominic. Dominic Brown. The kid from the Piggly Wiggly, pocketing gum, pretending to be a magician. Oh God.

I look at all six photographs. Yes, the curly hair and dark face, the small, quick hands. Not quick enough. Not capable of stopping bullets. I grab the reports. Why was he there?

According to a friend, Dominic had returned to school after it closed to retrieve a vocabulary list he needed for a spelling test the next day. Dominic snuck in the building through a half-open window near the gymnasium; his size-six sneakers left imprints beneath the sill. He never reached his locker. That required passing by the room where Marcus Rhodes lay screaming, begging, sobbing. Maybe Dominic thought he could help the man in trouble. Instead, he received a slug in the chest, ensuring that he would never learn how to spell "moustache." The vocabulary list is in a folder. I wonder if and how Ben plans to use it. It could prove an effective tool, gaining the jurors' sympathy. So cold, part of me thinks, acknowledging my analytic mind. Necessary, I think. Weeping at my desk isn't going to bring Dominic or Marcus back and it won't put their murderer away.

Marcus died second, or so they think. I imagine the bullets were a mercy, an end to the torment of the baseball bat that left splinters in his skull. You can see them in the close-ups, poking out like misplaced porcupine quills.

I read Emily Brown's statement. I can see her: the raindrops on her curls, her camel coat and small navy purse. She did not know her son had snuck out of the house. She admitted she would have punished him for forgetting his vocabulary list. He had done it twice before that same month. She would have grounded him and insisted he not play video games for a week. What this report omits is all that Emily Brown would give to have her son back, which is everything.

I smooth the sheet of paper as if I could take out the terrible wrinkles and make it whole. I cannot. All I can do is see that Calvin Washington pays for the crimes he committed. Reshuffling the photographs, I catch a glimpse of something I missed. There is a small matchbox car to the right of Dominic Brown's corpse. He was carrying it when Calvin Washington shot him. Did the tiny wheels of the car spin when they were jerked from his hand? I imagine the wheels spinning and in that hypnotic rotation I envision Calvin Washington strapped to a chair of death. The image does not disturb me. "I guess he'll die." The words surprise me. I did not intend to sing them, to think them, but there they are. "I guess he'll die."

Chapter Eleven

July 14, 2000

Friday night. Free at last. From my worn chintz seat I stare about my living room at the sofa, oversized chair, coffee table, television, mini-stereo, and a collection of end tables I cannot part with although I realize that five is too many for one room. The sofa's unblemished pale blue corduroy reveals that it is used for guest seating and that guests to my house are infrequent. I stare at my hazy reflection in the television's dead screen. I look limp, an abandoned rag doll. Only my hands are busy. One grasps a glass of iced tea, the other a telephone. I am prepared to leave a message. When a voice says, "Hello?" I almost spill my drink.

"Lacey?"

"Nat? Nat! How are you?" Her voice spikes with happiness. I tilt my head back to alleviate the pressure. Lacey's joy makes me ache. It's been that kind of day, that kind of week, that kind of life.

"I'm okay." I hesitate, then exhale. "No, I'm lying. I'm not."

"Goodness, are they teaching you how to lie down there? How very unlawyerly." Her teasing is familiar but the subject matter scratches like wool. I can never forget that the first casualty in my affair with Henry was Lacey. My first real lie told to her.

She had come downtown on an errand and swung by my office building to see if I wanted to have lunch. A surprise. She intercepted me as I was leaving the building with Henry. His hand rested lightly on the small of my back. It might have appeared mere chivalry. She smiled and explained she was just in the neighborhood. I introduced her to Henry. His glance didn't miss an inch of Lacey's lean frame, her golden hair, or her feline green-yellow eyes. It didn't bother me. Years of Lacey had inured me to the stares she garnered. She returned his gaze with frank curiosity and I could see her puzzling over him and who he was to me.

We invited her to join us for lunch but she declined. As she said "nice meeting you" to Henry I saw her look at his wedding ring. Her look at me asked, What are you doing, Nat? My unwavering smile and guilt-free face lied, Nothing, Lacey. I'm just having lunch, that's all. How could she know my transparent emotions had, in the course of my affair, become opaque? She later told me she knew I couldn't lie and she didn't expect I would, not to her. But I did, and she knows, and it hurts us both, still.

"So what's wrong?" Lacey asks, and I inhale, exhale, and inhale again before I can speak. Where to start?

"I've got my first murder trial coming up."

"But you've only been practicing for . . . how long?"

"Seven months. I'm only cocounsel. The original cocounsel, Jeffrey, quit the DA without so much as a by-your-leave. There are rumors that the pressure got to him. So I'm playing catch-up on a capital case. Ben Maddox is first chair."

"Isn't he the jerk who said that women ought to take the leave part of maternity leave to heart and stay home until their children go to college?" Her memory astonishes me sometimes.

"Yeah." I pull a curl from beside my ear because it tickles. I stretch the lock of hair until it can go no farther. Fully extended, it looks semistraight. I release it and the hair bounces back. "It's a death penalty case."

"Holy shit." She blurts the words.

"You can say that again."

"Well, honey, I can't say that you lead a quiet life. My God. Death penalty." I can see Lacey's wrinkled brow; she's reviewing all she knows on the death penalty. Her next question isn't procedural, but personal. "How is the family taking the news?"

"They don't know." I am matter-of-fact.

"Oh."

"Not really their cup of tea," I offer, failing at lightheartedness.

"I hope the death penalty isn't anybody's cup of tea, but . . ."

"What?"

"Well, not to be a bitch"—I smile, awaiting Lacey's pronouncement—"but your dad never clears his cases with you, does he? I mean, he doesn't always represent people you would want to lunch with."

This is an understatement. When I was twelve my father represented a local skinhead who displayed an enormous swastika on his front lawn and who leafleted cars and buildings with white-supremacy messages. Members of our synagogue asked my father why he had to represent a hateful man who embraced the very principles that had led to the murder of so many of their family members in Europe. My father said that everyone deserved the same First Amendment freedom-of-speech protections, no matter how offensive their message may appear. He explained why the man deserved representation, but avoided the real question. Why did *he* have to represent him?

I sigh and scissor my legs up and down. "Yeah, I'm not sure raising that point is going to win Mom and Dad over."

"When is the trial?"

"Not for a while. The unified appeals hearing took place two months ago, but we have to get a grand jury indictment before it goes to court for trial. It will be a couple of months." I sigh. "I saw one of the victims once, before he was killed. Well, obviously," I add. "He was only nine years old."

"Next time I start bitching about proofreading errors, feel free to slap me." Lacey works as an assistant editor in a publishing firm. Typos make her crazy; they always have.

The other troubling matter was the false Henry apparition, but I cannot speak of this. Lacey loathes Henry. She holds him responsible for the derailment of my career, the destruction of my dreams, and for taking me away from New York and her. In her world, blame must be assigned and the guilty party punished. She should have been the public prosecutor.

"So other than work, how is Georgia?"

"Peachy."

She laughs, a full, throat-warbling laugh. "Good one, Nat." And then, "So have you met anyone lately?" Here is where I do not tell her that I do not trust myself to meet anyone else.

"I meet men all the time at work."

"Yummy."

"Yeah, except I'm usually trying to convict them of crimes."

"I retract my yummy comment. Oh, but speaking of yummy, want to hear about my latest dating adventure? It began outside the Twenty-third Street Krispy Kreme." Lacey and doughnuts, like peanut butter and jelly, a duo for the ages.

"Do tell." I scrunch down farther in the chair and let my head rest against the arm.

"So I'd just come from a run—"

"In the park?" I interrupt.

"Yeah, and—"

"But the park is sixty blocks north of there." I know by "park" she means "Central."

"Yeah, but after doing my loop I was still feeling antsy so I decided to shake it up and run downtown a ways." Sixty blocks. Approximately four miles. And this after she ran three miles. Insane.

"So then I start heading to the West Side, and I realize my feet are leading me to Krispy Kreme, so I decide that my feet are geniuses and I obey and when I get there, of course, I'm a big, sweaty mess." No she wasn't. She was a lean running machine with heightened color and a dewy glow. "And when I get there there's this guy standing outside looking at the HOT NOW sign, which is unlit. He stares at it like it holds some sort of secret message, which made me think he might be nuts. But he was very cute."

"So you spoke to him."

"Of course. I mean, his attention was focused on that sign. He wasn't noticing anything around him." Including you, I almost say, but don't. Guys who ignore her intrigue Lacey because very few men do.

"So I say, 'Well, the HOT NOW sign is off, but if you go inside, the SORT OF WARM NOW sign is on.' And he turns to look at me and he is twenty times hotter than I thought and he says, 'It's ten-fifteen. The sign always goes on at ten. I've been waiting.' Then I start thinking, okay, he is superfine but he seems a little too committed to the Krispy Kreme clock, and perhaps I should return to my original opinion of crazy.

"So I am about to enter the building when I hear him scream 'Yes! Yes! I win!' behind me and I turn around and the sign is on and he is jumping up and down like a child."

"Certifiable," I remark.

"Then he turns to me and explains that he read an article about the Krispy Kreme dynasty and how all the chains are regulated to operate in a certain fashion, including when the HOT NOW sign goes on. But knowing New York, he figured the Twenty-third Street store would break the system at some point, so he and a friend made a bet on how long it would take for the system to fail. They picked the midmorning time and alternated vigils. Todd, that's the guy's name, was closest to the actual day."

"Does he have a job?" I ask, wondering how anyone would have the free time to develop such a theory, much less explore it.

"Yeah, he works for the Peace and Social Justice Division of the Ford Foundation."

"Nice. Very nice."

"Yeah, a man after your own heart. Fixing the world."

"So what happened after you determined he didn't belong in a rubber room?"

"I went inside for some doughnuts, and he came in, too. He ordered three sour-cream doughnuts." I have no doubt this meant something to Lacey. Divination by doughnut. "I sat down to eat mine and he sat across from me like he had known me from kindergarten and then he proceeds to tell me about Lou's Donuts in San Jose and how their maple-glazed cake doughnuts alone are worth the trip."

"Sure, a trip of three thousand miles for a doughnut."

"He did say it would be more worthwhile if you had business or family in the area. He does. Have family in the area, I mean."

"So you bonded over doughnuts. What then?"

"Well, I needed to get back to my place and shower, so I said it was nice meeting you and made leaving noises and motions and I thought he wasn't going to do anything. I mean, he just sat there, watching me through his glasses." Aha. Lacey is a sucker for men in glasses. "And I get up to go and he says, 'Do you like to dance?' "

"You're kidding." This is providential. Lacey loves dancing like she loves doughnuts.

"I said, 'Actually, yes,' and he sighs and says that will make the invitation he is about to extend more attractive, and I'm thinking what invitation? So then Todd invites me to this event featuring the Hubbard Street Dance Company, which was just awarded a grant by the Ford Foundation. There will be dinner, a show by the company, and then dancing."

"Did you accept?"

"Yes, but I'm a little nervous. It's going to be splashy. I don't know what to wear, and I barely know the guy."

"When is it?" Logistics are important to me.

"Next Friday night at the Ritz-Carlton, in their ballroom."

"So what does he look like?"

"Handsome, in that bookish way I love. Glasses. Blue eyes. Brown hair that's curly. Built, from what I could see. When he jumped up and down I got an eyeful of abs."

I laugh at the idea of Lacey checking out a guy she suspected might be crazy. "Atta girl," I tell her and add, "You should wear that long black dress with the strappy back."

"You think? It won't be too dressy?"

"Can you be overdressed in Manhattan?"

"True enough. The strappy black dress it is. That means heels. Good thing he's tall."

"You're going to have a great time. Hey, if the crazy doughnut guy doesn't work out, you can check out the dancers."

"Good idea."

Lacey deserves a good time.

"Hey Lacey, do you know if Deidre Kendall still runs a domestic abuse shelter?"

"I think so. No wait, yes, she does. I met someone recently who knew her and she said she still did. In Charleston. Why?"

"I've got a domestic abuse victim in need of help. It's a colleague's sister and he asked for my assistance. I told him I would see what I could do, and I thought maybe I would talk to Deidre and see what advice she has."

"Run and don't look back." Lacey sighs. "The world is a crap place sometimes, isn't it?"

"You can say that again."

"You want me to get Deidre's phone number and address for you?"

"That would be great. I feel guilty because I haven't done anything yet and I promised I would try to help." Even I can hear the expectation of failure in my voice.

"You're such a good person." Her tone implies that she, by contrast, is a disciple of Satan. "I'll get the info to you tomorrow." She sighs, deep and long and low. "I wish you still lived here. I spilled coffee on my new skirt and there was no one to tally my klutz points or offer me chocolate comfort." Lacey has accidents on a regular basis. I kept a running tally and even devised a rating system based on the degree of injury involved. Sometimes we would seek chocolate comfort to make her boo-boos better.

"I miss you, too. Call me after your big date and let me know how it went."

"I will. Love you, Nat."

"Love you, Lace."

"Bye."

I am alone again in my apartment. Staring at the ceiling, I appreciate that Lacey is able to take me out of myself, to wholly entertain and distract me. I tilt my head to the side to examine a small crack, just near the corner, or is that a cobweb? Lacey makes me less self-conscious whereas Henry made me self-aware every moment I spent with him. It was a bit exhausting. I suppose it's just as well that if I had to lose one of them it was Henry. Yes, it is a cobweb. And you know, it's obvious. If I lost one of them it would have to be Henry because Lacey would never abandon me, and that is what he did.

There were no telephone calls, no visits, no apologies. After I left the firm, I checked my answering machine and e-mail every half hour. By month's end I had hired movers to pack up and haul my belongings 950 miles south.

I managed to secure the job I had used to retaliate against those men: Walters, MacLittle, and Tate. Most especially Tate, who I knew did not believe me when I said I got a position as a prosecutor in Georgia. He thought he knew me too well. Knew the scar by my knee where I fell off my bike, knew my favorite ice cream—pistachio—and knew when I was bluffing about relocating to work in an unknown land. Getting the job had involved exaggerating my criminal law experience (clerking while in school) and calling on a favor from an old family friend, Walter Owens. In the seventies he and my dad had battled corrupt landlords and racist policemen together. Then my dad began getting some high-profile civil rights cases and Walter went his own way. He remembered me in pigtails and seemed surprised, though delighted, to hear from me.

He had moved to Georgia in 1985, and had risen to the ranks of judge in Atlanta. He said he would see what he could do. I hated asking for this favor, but not as much as I would hate not doing it. I had to do this, to prove I could.

On moving day I stood inside my empty Manhattan apartment and turned around once, committing the water-stained wood near the radiator and beautiful glass doorknobs to memory, afraid I might forget it all. I walked to my living room window and looked ten stories below to where summer-clad people hurried to their air-conditioned buildings. I exited my apartment and slammed the door, which set Mrs. Powalski's terrier to barking like a mad thing. I shrugged as I walked past. I wouldn't have to worry about Mrs. Powalski complaining about the noise level anymore, or her terrier, Henry James, who was noisier than any human in the building.

Four days after I moved, a package arrived from New York. Inside was a 1949 copy of Sidney Lanier's *The Marshes of Glynn* and a note. *Dearest Natalie, I am so very sorry. I hope you are able to forgive me someday. Yours, Henry.* I cried until my nose ran and then I cried some more. After I had wet half a box of tissues, I picked up the book to throw it across the room, but my arm held still. It wasn't the book's fault.

The package made me look for the photograph I had hidden inside my bedroom table. It was taken at an inn in upstate New York, during a rare stolen weekend. In it, we are seated together on a small bench on the inn's porch. Henry looks somber, his dark eyes wary, his posture rigid. I smile like a first-grader getting her school picture taken. That we are together is visible in our proximity, the way our bodies lean together, but that we are not truly together is visible in every other detail: his lack of smile, my too-bright grin, his hands gripped together, my own resting on my thighs, uncertain where to be if not around his torso, holding on.

Chapter Twelve

July 20, 2000

Carl and I have decided that a weekday is best. William will be working, and Carl's sister Sarah will be home with the children. I have driving directions, a road map, a bottle of water, and an orange that is making my car's interior smell like a citrus grove. The air conditioner blows cool air on my exposed arms, and while I am not eager to try to persuade Carl's sister to leave her husband, it is relaxing to be alone in my car, humming.

Just to be out of the office, away from Ben, is enough. We have been preparing for the grand jury hearing, and during these past days the scent of Ben's office, of leather and dust, has become too familiar. I have learned the names of the dead fish that hang on his walls and I am able to predict what he will eat for lunch. I have begun eating things I know will appall him for the pleasure of watching him grimace.

Ben's diet could use an overhaul. His prominent paunch, product of a meat-heavy, gravy-topped diet, makes me wonder if he knows what cholesterol is and how it works. Then again, most lawyers I know are crap eaters. They eat food that fits in their hand, on the go. Stuffing sandwiches and snack cakes into themselves with all the ceremony of a person stuffing quarters into a Laundromat washing machine.

The bright green exit sign for 167B is ahead. I recall my conversation with Deidre Kendall, of the statistics she gave me on domestic abuse and the common reactions to anticipate. Deidre was patient and kind, but realistic. She cautioned me that my intervention might gain me nothing but hostility. "That's okay," I had told her. "I'm a public prosecutor. Hostility comes with the territory."

"I heard rumors you had moved South to do public law. That's great." Her sincerity made me cringe. I thanked her for her help and wished her luck in her own work.

Savannah is beautiful. The downtown is divided into grids punctuated by small gardens and squares, the epitome of good city planning. However, many of these streets are marked one way, making the grid into a maze. I have to make a third right before I reach the street that will take me to East Broad, where Sarah lives, on the fringe of the fashionable historic district. I slow and begin reading the numbers on the houses. Sixty-four, sixty-six. I am close. My stomach stirs and I realize I forgot to pack antacids. Eighty-four. I park in the adjoining driveway behind a brown minivan.

The house is postcard pretty: white wood with ivy-green shuttered windows and a brick walkway that intersects grass so lush it looks fake. The doorbell ding-dongs, causing a dog inside to bark, fast and angry. I almost slip off the low cement stair in my hurry to step backward. Carl didn't warn me about a dog.

When the door opens it reveals a younger, female Carl and a petite terrier. My embarrassment renders me speechless, allowing Sarah to ask, "Can I help you?" Her tone implies that she would prefer I say no and leave. This, plus the fading bruise on her cheekbone, assures me that I have found the right woman and the right house.

"Sarah Henning? My name is Natalie Goldberg. I work with your brother Carl."

"Carl?" Her voice, anxious, sounds like Carl's, only a little higher and softer. "Is he okay?"

"He's fine. That's not why I'm here. May I come in?" So what if I sound like a pushy Northerner? I am one.

Her face wrinkles with worry, revealing a crease mark in her makeup. Through it I see the faded outline of another bruise on her temple. I suspect that without cosmetics she might resemble an Impressionist painting, all swirls of color, applied with fists, not brushes.

Sarah steps backward. I accept her silent invitation before she can reconsider. She walks past a pristine foyer that smells of wood polish into a sitting room filled with antique furniture, including a cabinet of violet-patterned china plates and teacups. This furniture would pass a white-glove test. The children must be barred from this room. Where were they? The house was silent, no pitter patter of little feet audible.

"You said Carl is okay?" Her determination to make sure reminds me of Carl and makes me smile. Her eyes are brown, not blue, but her teeth are just as white-picket perfect.

"Yes, he is well. I came because he mentioned that you're in need of help." A progression of emotions alters her face: confusion, anger, embarrassment, then fear, and finally the tight mask she should have worn if she wanted to fool me. Not that she could. The makeup, the bruises, and the too tidy home: it all speaks of abuse, as did her silence. Silence is the native language of abuse.

"Carl is mistaken." She clears her throat. "I do not require assistance. I am sorry you took time out of your schedule to come by on an unnecessary errand." Her brown eyes meet mine.

My fists clench. Errand? Errand? She describes my three-hour drive to her house to rescue her and her children as an errand? As if it were no more than emptying the trash or cleaning the tub?

"Whether you believe it or not, you need help. Those fading black and blue marks will be replaced by fresh marks or broken bones." She touches her cheek. "Your children may very well be visiting the same emergency rooms you frequent unless your husband is clever enough to rotate visits to different hospitals." I tilt my head to the side, and she flinches at this prediction.

"Billy and Lily are at an exceptionally high risk. In homes where partner abuse occurs, children are fifteen hundred times more likely to be abused." Her shoulders hunch. "Plus they are learning behavior that could influence them. According to the American Psychological Association Presidential Task Force on Violence and the Family, a child's exposure to the father abusing the mother is the strongest risk factor for transmitting violent behavior from one generation to the next. Billy might hit his own girlfriend or wife. He'll think it's normal, that daddies hit mommies, that men beat women."

She sniffles and shakes her head, but I don't stop. "Fifty percent of all women murdered are killed by their spouses or an acquaintance." I throw facts and statistics at her until her tight face crumples in on itself. Then I lean forward and hand her a portable packet of Kleenex and feel like an absolute monster.

No kindness or empathy. No. I went straight into my bad-cop routine. And all because she demeaned my act of compassion by calling it an errand. Deidre warned me she might be hostile but did I pay attention? Guilt makes me feel five hundred pounds heavier. I listen to the grandfather clock tick until she stops crying. Then I tell her what she should do next: leave with the children, go to the police station and file charges, get a restraining order. Drive to the nearest shelter and stay there until we can begin legal proceedings.

"You'll divorce him," I say, "and you'll be safe. We'll keep you and Billy and Lily safe." I don't mention the other statistic about battered women: that they are more likely to be killed when leaving their abuser.

I fold clothes for Sarah and she settles them into suitcases. "He used to be sweet," she tells me. I recognize the instinct to defend one's worst choices.

"I'm sure he was," I say. Sarah hands me clothing, a bag of toiletries, and, at my suggestion, some bedding.

"Shelters are often overcrowded," I say. She nods but I see the fog of doubt cloud her eyes. She is wondering what she has consented to, what this shelter will be like.

We collect the children from the house next door. Sarah introduces me to her neighbor as Jessica, an old high school friend. We don't want to leave an easy trail for William. The woman rests a hand on Sarah's arm and asks if she knows what she is doing. I place my hand on Sarah's shoulder. "She does now," I tell the woman, daring her to defy me. I would like her to, so that I could argue with her, ask why the hell she let her friend and neighbor get hit night after night. She must see the anger in my eyes, for she says nothing.

Billy has a snub nose I assume comes from William. Lily has Sarah's flaxen hair. They bounce about, high on lemonade and summertime fun. We interrupted their water balloon fight. They need dry clothes before setting out on their trip, which they want to know all about. Where are we going? Why? When will we be back? Could they give Captain a dog treat before they leave? Sarah's eyes grow damp, but I shake my head no. Shelters don't allow pets. I don't envy the dog, alone in a house with an abandoned, enraged

William, but there is no time to plan around him. William is due home in five hours and so much remains to be done.

"Sarah, I need you to do one last thing." She is holding Lily's favorite bear, Mr. Cuddles.

"What?" She sounds doubtful. I cannot blame her.

"Wash your face."

"What?"

I imagine she hasn't left the house without cosmetics in years, but it will make our entry into the police station easier by clearing any doubt from skeptical cops' minds about what is happening at 84 East Broad Street.

I carry the last suitcase downstairs and pack it into the rear of the minivan. Sarah emerges a few moments later. Her face is wet and red, as if she scrubbed hard and fast with a washcloth. The right side is a palette of bleeding colors, blues into purples into lime greens. The left side is unmarred except for a small scar by her eye. Holding the teddy bear heightens the impression of a funhouse mirror: distorted and frightening.

Lily looks at her mother and says, "Why are you practicing for Halloween?"

Billy says nothing; he knows his mother isn't playing a game.

The policemen at the station are kind. They distract the kids with coloring books and an abbreviated tour of the station (no occupied jail cells or weapons closets inspections). It charms and dismays me; how comfortable they are with the children, an ease won from too many similar visits. I sit beside Sarah, interjecting legal advice when needed, which isn't often. The legal battles will follow.

On our way out of the station a cop taps his dark hand against my shoulder. "Hey, aren't you the daughter of the guy who represented Clinton Fellows?" Clinton was famous in Georgia for protesting unequal real estate pricing for blacks during the 1980s. I remembered him as a soft-spoken man who always carried hard candies in his pockets.

I tell the policeman that Aaron Goldberg is my father.

"Following in your old man's footsteps, huh? That's great."

"Not exactly. I'm a public prosecutor."

The cop, who could not have been more than fifteen when Clinton was on trial, ignores my heavy voice. "But you're helping people, right? You're helping this lady and her kids." He nods toward Sarah and her wide-eyed children.

"Sure," I say.

When I was five years old I wanted to be Wonder Woman. I had the Underoos and a long loop of rope and a pair of tall boots borrowed from my mother's closet. I dashed through the house, clad in star-spangled splendor, ready to right wrongs. While I usher Sarah and the kids outside I find myself wishing I still had those Underoos. Not that they would fit, but I crave the feeling of invincibility and magic they provided. When I wore them I was better than my everyday self.

On the highway, I watch the rearview mirror to check that Sarah is still following me. She could skip. Nothing is preventing her from turning off at the next exit, returning to her life. No matter how awful, it is familiar.

When I outgrew my Underoos I wore a costume shop set of fake glasses/nose and carried a briefcase, sporting a pilfered suit jacket that hung below my knees. My second hero? My father. When did I outgrow that costume?

After twenty-six miles of buzzing highway it is time to turn off and head to the shelter. My directional click-clacks. In the mirror I see Sarah has hers on, as well. She will follow me this far at least. Thank God for that.

Chapter Thirteen

July 29, 2000

This is just what the doctor ordered. Actually, it is just what Lala ordered. She told me I should visit the State Botanical Garden in Athens, and then she wrote out directions in a swirly, frail script. I invited her to come along, but she declined. It is a two-hour trip to Athens, and Lala tries to limit her travel radius to fifteen minutes from her white clapboard home. I wonder if she began this policy after her husband's driving-related death. It may be that she doesn't like long car trips.

The sloping walkways of the shade garden twist and turn around sections named in honor of the seven districts of the garden clubs of Georgia. Here the trees block the merciless sun's rays. The last thermometer I passed registered 87 degrees, but I am certain it broke, unable to cope with another hot and humid day. I look into the pool at the Mathis Plaza, at the reflected trees, and recall Lala in her straw hat and pink and green plaid Bermuda shorts, waving me Godspeed on my journey to Athens. I should have told her not to worry. If the past week hadn't killed me, nothing could.

Contrary to my expectations, the grand jury hearing went well. Ben did all the talking. I sat in the air-conditioned room during the two-day proceedings, taking notes and watching the faces assembled in the conference room. Georgia law requires that the grand jury be balanced in terms of race and sex with respect to the county's population as determined by the last census and the number of persons in each jury pool. Of the twenty-one jurors assembled, twelve were female, ten male. Twelve were black, nine white. None of them prevaricated before returning a true bill indicting Calvin Washington for murder, felonious murder, and aggravated assault. We didn't get the simple majority required of an indictment. We got each and every juror.

Each grand juror in Georgia is sworn thus: *You shall present no one from envy, hatred, or malice, nor shall you leave anyone unpresented from fear, favor, affection, reward, or the hope thereof, but you shall present all things truly and as they come to your knowledge. So help you God.* For "present" read "indict" or "convict." I admire this oath because it recognizes human frailty and the temptations of power that must be avoided in exercising justice. The seventeen people assembled around the large oval table watched Ben. They listened to his statements and asked careful questions. They knew what returning an indictment meant. I could only hope we would acquire an equally thoughtful jury for the criminal trial.

My garden map is wrinkled and damp. The public grounds comprise a tiny portion of the 313-acre preserve the state botanical garden includes, and I would hate to lose my way. I turn away from the shaded paths, determined to brave the cruel sun for a stroll through the International Garden. The map illustration promises geometric-patterned gardens. It sounds like my kind of space.

Sweaty half-moons are forming beneath my armpits. My face crackles with heat, and I know that despite a liberal dose of sunscreen and my Boston Red Sox baseball cap, I am going to have a dotting of freckles on and around my nose by day's end. I imagine them sprouting to the surface like eager seedlings. Freckles make me look younger, contradicting my work attire of ironed garments, coordinated jewelry, and deep red lipstick. I rub my nose as if I can somehow stop the forming freckles.

The shade garden gives way to an open path spotted with knee-high plaques that give the flowers' Latin names, growing season, and interesting facts. I learn that *Sedum spectabile* "Herbstfreude," known as "Autumn Joy," attracts honeybees and butterflies with its clusters of red-pink flowers. My focus is diluted by droplets of sweat that threaten to run into my eyes and the image of Sarah, who has been playing hide-and-seek in my mind since I saw her nine days ago. She appears at unexpected moments, much like her brother Carl. He tells me she and the kids are still at the shelter, still safe. He does not tell me that they are frightened or confused, but I can imagine.

The International Garden exceeds my hopes. Among the designed flower plots is a garden with herbs used in the Middle Ages for dyes, cooking, and medicines. The air smells cooler and tangier here. I bend down and breathe deeply, the fragrances filling my sinuses, blocking the smell of sunscreen and sweat. I distinguish lavender, which is supposed to promote relaxation. I could use some.

The curved benches beside the herbs are just what my tired legs need. I lean back against the wood, exhale, and close my eyes. If I breathe hard enough perhaps I can distinguish the scent of photosynthesis. I smile and open my eyes. A dark blur in front of me resolves itself into the shape of a woman. She wears the tan shorts and button-down shirt of a garden employee. She smiles at me, the rest of her features hazy with sun. "Looks like you're enjoying the garden," she says.

"It's wonderful."

She looks about her, at the boxed growths of grouped plants and flowers. "It sure is. You have a nice day." She walks toward the visitors' center, her steps light and brisk despite the heat.

I have grown more accustomed to people talking to me unprompted, a culture shock after New York, where strangers don't speak to you unless it's to share advice like "get the fuck out of the way." The unexpected kind comment, the sincere wish for another's happiness, still catches me off guard. At least it's a happy surprise, a nice moment, unlike yesterday's bombshell from Ben.

We sorted the physical evidence, reviewing what Wilkins and Cox had told us, when Ben said he needed to leave early that evening. Surprised that he would bother to tell me, I shrugged. "An old friend is in town." Alarm bells should have rung in my skull, for Ben didn't share personal details of his life any more than I did. "Walter Owens. We went to school together. He is a judge."

That's when the fire alarm inside my head shrieked, too late. "You know Judge Owens, don't you?" His eyes lasered me, his hands resting on his paunch. "He recommended you for this job."

Yes, at my behest, Judge Owens recommended me for this job. My chest felt as if a boa constrictor were hugging me. How much did Ben know?

"I will be sure to tell him how you are doing," he promised, tilting back farther in his chair. If he wasn't careful, he would tip too far and fall to the floor. If I were lucky his skull would split like a cantaloupe.

"And how would that be?" My voice, flat and cool, cost me some effort.

A light flared within Ben's eyes. Anger? Admiration? Surprise? "You're learning," he said. "You're getting a lot of court exposure."

Such high praise, I almost said, but didn't. I was afraid to annoy him. He knew something about me, or did he? Judge Owens's connection to my hiring wasn't a secret but the link between that and my leaving New York was, or so I had believed. Did Ben know something about the circumstances under which I had left Walters, MacLittle, and Tate or was he irked that I had been hired, in part, because of friendly influence? He has never made bones about his feelings that my gender, privilege, and education annoy him. Perhaps Judge Owens'a alliance also needles him and that is all he meant. I don't know, and it's still driving me mad, four days later.

I shake my head to clear it of the questions I cannot answer and look about me. Few people walk among the fragrant paths. They probably decided that a late July afternoon might not be the best time to be out-of-doors. They may be cooler but they're missing the buzz of honeybees swarming about bright blossoms. Their fat black and yellow bodies fly in inebriated patterns, affected by the heat, or maybe the environment. So many flowers in one place. It is honeybee paradise.

I rise from my seat and wander anew. I stop reading the plaques. The visual input is enough. If only I could keep the other thoughts at bay, the worries, the pain. It is both worse and better than when I first arrived, numb with grief. In those first months I did nothing but unpack, study, assist on cases, study and then study some more. With the bar exam over I worked more than necessary and decorated my new rental and kept everyone at arm's length. Now it's getting complicated with the casework and the death penalty and Ben's veiled hints and Carl's abused sister and missing things like Lacey and the easy relationship I once had with my parents.

Although I haven't visited the dahlia garden yet, I decide it is time to leave. The distraction of the gardens has passed. As I cross the parking lot I wonder if perhaps I should go into therapy, and then I snort a half-laugh because the craziest people I know are the ones who became therapists. Lacey says psychiatrists take comfort in their work because it validates their own insanity.

In my rearview mirror I can see the high gates surrounding the state garden. An enormous painted wooden flower summons nature lovers. The fake blossom is bright yellow and orange and so big that I am a half-mile away before it fades from sight, its cheerful petals disappearing behind a slow-grade hill.

"Good-bye, gardens," I say, and then I turn the radio on and search for something to sing along to, something bright and silly to match the freckles radiating from my nose out to my cheeks like a pioneer girl doll's.

Chapter Fourteen

August 9, 2000

Ben is hiding something. He has been out of the office several times. I know he has not been tied up in court. I would know if he had other hearings scheduled. More unsettling is his apologetic tone when he says, "I'll be out tomorrow." He seems almost guilty, certainly furtive. Could he be having an affair? Is this why his wife stopped by his office? To make sure he was at work?

He is out today, again, and I should be celebrating. I can concentrate on my cases without worry of interruption, of impromptu quizzes on everything from police procedure to appeals, of needless comments on my organization system. Ben is a piler. He has stacks of paper in his office, on his desk, his floor, and his chairs. He can locate the items he needs, though I have no idea how he does it. His office looks like a life-sized game of Legal Jenga. One false move and the entire system could topple.

Once, when I reached into my birthday tickler file to extract a thank-you card, Ben coughed several times before managing to ask, "You have a greeting card organizer?"

"Sure." I opened the plastic folder's expanding mouth so that he could see each slot marked by month. "I buy birthday cards in advance and file them by month. I have extras for things like 'get well' and 'thank you' cards. It's great. I never run to the drugstore and panic because I can't find an appropriate card, and I'm never late mailing them."

He laughed and choked at the same time. When he recovered he told me, "You're a little scary."

"Just a little?" I asked.

Ben walked away, muttering "anal retentive" under his breath. I smiled before licking the thank-you card's matching lilac envelope. It didn't look as though Ben was going to adopt my filing system anytime soon.

To my surprise he asked me about it a few days later. "What do you call it?"

"The birthday tickler file."

"Why tickler?" His morbid fascination needed appeasing.

"Because it tickles your memory." Unable to resist, I added, "Or your fancy. You want to go card-shopping during lunch?" His wide-eyed horror was all the reward I sought. "Let me know if you change your mind."

Okay, so we're not a super duo, but we were making progress in communicating. Only now he is gone, again, and I don't know why. I try to push the matter aside with a mental bulldozer. I stare at the sheaf of papers comprising my latest assignment: an arson case involving no corpses and no injuries, just a razed building insured for four hundred thousand dollars. I should be delighted. The outraged parties are: the insurers, who don't want to cut a check for a building they suspect was torched by the owner's nephew, and the firefighters who claim that the fire could have consumed nearby residential buildings. I find this hard to care about. It doesn't compel me. It's too much like the faceless paper-pushing work I did in New York where the only things at stake were varying amounts of money and sometimes a multibillion-dollar company's reputation. I need something more. Good God, I sound like a pain junkie. I run a hand through my hair, catching my fingers in a cluster of curls.

Carl walks in as I am attempting to remove my hand from my hair. "Hi, Nat," he says. "May I talk to you?"

"Sure." I pull my fingers free, ripping some hairs from my scalp. I swallow a scream and brush the hairs into my wastebasket. My father's hair is a genetic curse.

"I just wanted to update you on Sarah and the kids." He rubs his large hands up and down the tops of his legs, from his thighs to his kneecaps. "They've moved out of the shelter and are staying with our mom's sister, Aunt Jemima."

"You have an Aunt Jemima?" I envision a black woman wearing a spotted kerchief atop her head, smiling down from a bottle of maple syrup.

"Yeah. I know. The name. We call her Jemmy. Everyone does. Anyway, they're with her in Vidalia. William tried to file some custody papers, claiming that Sarah is mentally unstable and unfit to parent." He chafes his legs harder.

"I assume his petition was denied?"

"Yes. So far his attempts to get the kids back have failed. The police in Savannah were impressed by your visit. Their report made clear to the judge that William shouldn't get near her or the kids for now."

"Good." I remember leaving Sarah at the shelter. She tried to hide the tremor in her hands from Billy and Lily, who wanted to know why the house was set so far into the woods. The better to hide you from your father, I thought, but did not say. I left it to Sarah to explain.

"I can't thank you enough for your help."

Oh, but he could, and he had. I had heard nothing but "thank you" from Carl since I returned that day, wanting to bury myself under my sheets and sleep the rest of the week.

"Really, Carl, like I said, she was ready to go. I just nudged her." "Pushed her" is more accurate; pushed her like a mother bird pushes its baby out of the nest. Fly or die.

"She left because of you. I know it." He reaches into his interior jacket pocket and withdraws a long flat box of gray velvet, a jeweler's box. He sets it onto the desk and pushes it toward me. "This is a thank-you gift. My mother helped pick it out." There is only a mother. Carl's father died years ago of a heart attack.

I reach forward, hesitant. The box lid lifts with a small snap. Inside, a bright coil of silver is laid out and in its midst lies a tiny chai, the Jewish symbol for life. "It's beautiful," I murmur. Wherever did he find this?

"Do you like it?" He looks from the necklace to me and then back to the necklace.

I touch the small silver symbol, the Hebrew letters Chet and Yod attached. Is it me or does it feel warm? "Yes. Thank you. You know, you didn't have to get me anything."

"I wanted to and my mother wanted to, as well. Sarah and Billy and Lily mean so much to us."

I finger the slender thread of silver. Carl rises and asks, "Do you need help putting it on?"

"No," I say. "No, that's okay. I can do it myself." My office door is open. What if someone walked by and saw Carl fastening a necklace about my neck? They would not understand. I fasten the clasp and smooth the chain, trying to soothe myself.

"Looks pretty." He displays his perfect teeth for me in a wide smile.

"Yes, it does." The chai rests above the cleft of my breasts.

I ask him how his caseload is and he says everything is fine, and his packing is almost done. Of course, he is uncertain he should go on vacation with Sarah's situation unresolved. I tell him the situation won't be resolved for some time and that he deserves the trip to Bermuda. He leaves after thanking me twice more.

I do not tell him I could use a vacation from his well-meaning inquiries, from his gratitude and his gift.

Henry gave me a ruby ring surrounded by delicate gold filigree. It overwhelmed the fourth finger of my right hand. Of course, it could not be made to fit my left ring finger. That would have raised questions at the office. When I left New York, I took the ring with me. It sits in a box tucked amid lacy underthings I wear when I have run through my clean cotton panties and do not have the time or the inclination to do laundry.

Now there is Carl's necklace. Some women would give their eyeteeth to have handsome men offer them jewelry. Not me. I just want an untarnished professional reputation. I should have considered that before I followed Henry into that hotel room. But I could not see beyond the moment, beyond the tread of his leather shoes on that thick carpet, leading me forward to something new.

I run the charm from side to side on the slender silver chain, back and forth, back and forth. The chai makes a small humming noise as it slides against the chain. Carl's gift came with a physical tic; how appropriate. I still my hand and look toward my chirping computer. It reminds me I have a plea-bargain discussion in an hour with Helen Leland. Her client shot up a convenience store during a robbery, but the only thing he hit was a freezer full of ice cream. The cops reached him before he could get anything into his pockets other than a package of licorice. Sadly, ineptitude is not a mitigating circumstance, not in my book.

I am contemplating how best to needle Helen about the candy

thief. Something like, "Maybe your client should have practiced stealing from babies. I hear it's pretty easy."

Will interrupts, popping his head in and rapping his knuckles on the frame, rather than the door.

"Hi, Will."

"Have you got a minute?"

"Sure. I'm just preparing to tell Helen Leland that her client's idiocy doesn't qualify as a mental defect."

His weary face reshapes itself as he smiles. The pockets of sleeplessness beneath his hazel eyes disappear and his ears lift like those of a happy puppy. "The licorice thief?" I nod. He knows. Of course he does. Will tries to keep abreast of everything. Hence the eye pouches.

"What can I do for you?" I ask.

"Nothing. At least nothing you're not already doing." His tone implies that he recognizes that I'm overworked and underpaid, but that we're all in this boat together. "I actually wanted to talk about the Washington case."

Will closes the door behind him before taking a seat opposite me. Uh-oh.

"How are things going?" Will steeples his fingers together. It's his office chief pose. It does not augur glad tidings.

"Fine. Good. We have a lot of physical evidence and plenty of witnesses to testify to the fight between Calvin and Marcus. It's a solid case." "Solid" is one step below "a lock" but I won't use that term about this case. I almost never use it. "A lock" implies there is no way you can lose, and as any trial lawyer will tell you, there are more ways to lose a case than you thought possible.

"I'm glad to hear it. And you? How are you holding up?"

"You mean how do I feel about assisting a prosecution that might result in a man's death?"

Will raises his pointed index fingers to his lips and nods.

"I should buy stock in Maalox, given the amount I've consumed the past few weeks." Will says nothing. "You know I oppose the death penalty, but this is my job, and I believe in justice. It's up to the jurors ultimately."

"You're right. It is up to the jurors. It's a tremendous responsibility. The administration of criminal justice. Alexander Hamilton called it 'the great cement of society.' "

"He also wrote that the states' power to administer criminal and civil justice independent of other influences could so wholly wield power over their citizens as to prove a threat to the power of the Union."

Will's lips curl upward. Silent praise. "You like *The Federalist Papers*?"

"Quite a lot. I wrote a paper in law school citing Number 17. A paper on the death penalty and the states' abuse of power in using it, but somehow, I think you already know that."

Will nods. "Good paper. A little heavy on philosophy citations, but good."

"I'm glad you enjoyed it." I had not suspected Will read anything I wrote in law school, but I maintain a veneer of calm. I resist the urge to tap my feet, to betray my nervousness.

"You're a bright girl, Natalie, and I'm glad we got you." He makes me sound as if I was the number one draft pick for a sports team. "You passed your multistate bar exam with how many months to prepare?"

"Three." But it was all I did. Burning the letters of the law into my brain helped keep me from picking up the phone and screaming at Henry or filing a civil suit against Walters and MacLittle. Not that I would have won. It was their word against mine.

"Three months. Wow. I'm glad we were able to get your fitness paperwork processed in time. I would have hated to make you wait until the February exam, although at first I thought you would have done well to wait." Will had tried to convince me to postpone taking the bar exam. He said I could assist for a few more months before taking it. He was a little afraid I would fail. Not as afraid as I was.

"My fitness certificate?" As I recalled, that had been done within weeks.

"Yes. Normally you have to submit the fitness certificate and have it approved seven months before you can apply to the bar."

I hear a low buzz, as if a mosquito is whining by my ear. I look to my shoulder but there are no insects nearby.

"Seven months?" I repeat, sure I must have misheard.

"Well, that's the usual. Four months for those who wait until the last moment." He smiles as if we share a common tendency to postpone things. "Good thing you knew you wanted to come here, and Judge Owens was able to help out." My smile is weak.

"He's a good man, despite his shoes." Will invites me to laugh with him, to mock Judge Owens's footwear. He does not realize that I cannot recall what Judge Owens wears on his feet. Sandals? Cowboy boots? "He was able to push it through the Bar Admissions Committee, since he serves on it."

The fitness certificate is required of all lawyers who wish to practice in Georgia. You must submit it before taking the bar. But by seven months! I had no idea, though Judge Owens did, thank God. Everyone in Georgia must know, including Ben. Shit. Will's voice is tinny and distant and I realize I have missed the first part of his sentence when he says, "Ben tell you?"

I shake my head to clear the buzzing and the dark suspicions that have begun to sprout within my mind, poisonous seeds. "Pardon?" I say.

"He didn't, did he?" He sighs, an atypical vocalization of displeasure. "Ben has prostate cancer."

"What?" I don't mean to yell, but the syllable explodes from my mouth.

"He was diagnosed two months ago. He went for a routine physical and the doctor noticed something wrong."

I am trying to wrap my head around what he is telling me while attempting to banish the image of Ben in a hospital gown being examined from behind.

"He has stage two cancer. He is scheduled to go in for radiation treatment. It's a simple operation." Will is staring at the law books behind me with singular focus. "He goes next week. He should be out of the hospital in a day, but I have ordered him out of the office for a week. I think he should rest, and make sure he is fit to return to work." He directs his eyes my way, able to look at me now that he has finished discussing Ben's prostate. "I had hoped he would mention it to you."

My God. Cancer. That was why his wife looked so concerned in his office that day. He wasn't having an affair.

"I know he and you don't see eye to eye on everything."

A sandpaper scrap of laughter escapes. "You could say that," I say. "But we've made some progress . . . or I thought we had . . . the case preparations are going well," I conclude, aware of how lame my words sound. How well could we be communicating if Ben hasn't told me about his illness?

"I suspected Ben hadn't told you, though I urged him to. I realize it's a private matter, but you are teamed on this case, and I don't have to remind you of its importance. I thought you should know."

"Sure." What is there to say? I rest my elbows on the reliable weight of Guvnor's solid wood desk.

"Ben is a good lawyer. Old-fashioned and a bit opinionated, but solid. We're lucky to have him. I think he can teach you quite a bit." Will smiles to make this more palatable. "And I'm sure you can impart an idea or two into his mind."

"Easier said than done."

"Who was it that said anything easy isn't worth having?"

"Someone spoiled since birth?" I would give my right eye for things easily achievable at this moment.

He rises from the chair with a wince, as if sitting so long has done him injury. "I hope you'll forgive me for bringing you bad news, but I did think you ought to know about Ben."

"Thanks for telling me."

"He's not a bad guy." "Bad guy" wasn't the term I was looking to apply.

"You know Jeff's leaving had nothing to do with him, right?" I blink hard, appalled that Will intuited my darkest thoughts about Ben. At my most frustrated I have wondered if he was responsible for Jeffrey's departure from our offices. I nod acknowledgment.

"Is it okay to tell him I know?" I ask, although I have no idea how I will.

"Yes. I think it would be best."

I think it would be best for Will to leave now, before he can impart any more awful news. He does, with a somber "I'm sorry" and a more cheerful "Have fun with the candy thief."

I rest my face in the cradle of my palms, aware that I have to meet Helen in less than half an hour. I cannot seem to move, buried under a tide of unexpected news. My torso shakes, as if cold. I lift my face to stare across the room at my suit jacket, hanging upon its hook. The deep blue of the fabric looks almost like a cutout in the door's shiny wood, as though someone had sawed a hole in the shape of a hanging jacket in the door. I could put my hand through it and feel . . . what? I do not know, but whatever lies behind seems preferable to what lies on this side of the door. There is no escape on this side, only more secrets. I can delay pondering them, though, and I must if I am going to meet Helen in twenty minutes. The candy thief jokes I had prepared seem stale now, soured by the dark emotions Will deposited in my office.

Chapter Fifteen

Someone from the Spring Street frame shop left me a message that my pictures are ready. I had planned to wait until tomorrow to pick them up, but while driving home I change my mind. This displeases the driver behind me who yells, "Learn how to drive!" in reaction to my abrupt left turn. In Georgia, drivers yell at you. They don't lean on their horns as New Yorkers do or flip you the finger as Bostonians do or shoot you with their handguns as Los Angelenos do. They shout out their window. I think it's a more personal expression of road rage.

A bald-headed man inside the shop is turning the OPEN sign to CLOSED as I reach the door. He grins and turns it over again, ushering me inside with a "You picking something up?" I give him my name and he disappears into the back room I imagine stocked high with paintings and posters and photographs.

I study matting materials and rulers and cutting instruments until the man reappears, his arms stretched wide around a bulky package of brown paper tied with twine, the pale, wiry sort capable of cutting you. I imagine getting home and untying the string to find velvet Elvis paintings or *Dogs Playing Poker* inside.

"They're lovely works," he says, tapping the paper with a forefinger stained blue. He hesitates before asking, "Is the girl in the drawing . . . is that you?"

How to answer this? "My sister," I say. I have found the phantom sibling I always wanted.

"That explains the resemblance."

The package is heavy. I carry it with extended arms, trying my best not to knock it against doorways, tables, or chairs. Huffing and puffing, I resolve to join a gym, any gym, someday soon. I set it on the kitchen table and fetch a steak knife. My purse swings back and forth, a leather pendulum below my arm, as I saw at the package's string. It snaps with a soft pop. I fold back the crisp brown paper, and there she is, my sister of the laughing eyes and dimpled cheek, framed in gilt scalloped wood. The painting looks almost alive. I half expect her to speak to me, but she remains silent and I transfer her to a chair so that I may look at the second picture.

It is a small oil painting bought late last summer during a street fair. I kept passing back and forth before an artist's stand until he asked, "See anything you like?" I did. A picture of blue hydrangeas painted on Masonite. He wanted less than I would have paid, so little I thought I misheard him. I told Lacey about my purchase and predicted that if she ever left New York she would be confronted by reverse sticker shock.

"It's bad enough you moved away. Now you have to tell me how cheap things are elsewhere? Gee, thanks," she said. I made sure never to disclose how little I pay in rent for my house after that conversation.

I pause before lifting the second picture to reveal the third item, the one I hesitated over before adding it to the "to be framed" pile.

It is a diptych. In the left photograph I stand, hip high to my father, before the wrought iron of Johnston Gate at Harvard. My mother took this picture one July day when we walked about the square. I rode atop my father's shoulders; my pigtails bounced as he walked. We stopped and my mother pointed through the bars of the tall black gate that looked as if it belonged in the pages of my fairy-tale book. Beyond the gate were green lawns and curvy footpaths and dark redbrick buildings.

"That's where your dad went to school." Even before she said it, I longed to go inside, to chase the squirrels and to pretend to read like the man sitting on the steps of the building across from us.

"I'm going to go to school here, too," I said, bending forward so that my father could see my face. He groaned and swung me over and down, into his arms. He squeezed me, so tight I thought my chest would burst like a balloon.

"Of course you will," he said.

The photograph on the right shows me shoulder high to my father, gowned and capped in black, my diploma gripped in my left hand. We stand before the same gate. Captured again are the broad smiles and the sun-inspired squints. We are happy. I rub my eyes, refusing to be sidetracked by regret. I rewrap the paper around the pictures and move the stack to the counter. Out of sight . . . well, out of sight. Inside the refrigerator I search for comfort. I find left-over barbecue. It will do.

The tang of the barbecue sauce comes as a pleasant departure from my menu of frozen dinners. I offer a silent thank-you to Lala, who pressed the remains of her church's barbecue feast on me. Lala says it is a pity I keep such long hours, and never have time to cook. Yes, I tell her, I could really use a wife: someone to cook and clean for me so when I get home supper is on the table, someone like my mother. Though cooking was never her strength.

I munch on a salted corncob. Back in the area of my brain where memories collect cobwebs, I see my grandpapa rubbing his corncob into a stick of butter, transforming its solid surface into a molten crater pocked with kernels. Did his wife scold him, or was she gone by then? I try to remember, staring at the rippled surface of the butter stick before me in which one kernel stands, legacy of my grandpapa. He died when I was eight. By age ten, all my grandparents had passed away, leaving little but furniture and photographs and memories I must turn over and examine, checking for authenticity.

I could call my parents and ask, "Did Grandpapa always roll his corn in the butter or did he do it to amuse me?" They too might not remember. Long ago our family circle constricted to include only we three. I wipe a smear of barbecue sauce from the rim of my plate and suck the sauce from my finger. Two and one, I think, not three. I am outside that circle now.

"Don't play with your food, Natalie," I can hear my father's deep voice intone as I make a face with corn kernel eyes, macaroni ears and nose, and a half-biscuit mouth. He would scold me when he was tired or upset and noticed me arranging my food into pictures or rainbow spectrums. If his cases were going well, if he was distracted with thoughts of writing a speech for the New England Chapter of the American Civil Liberties Union, he would not scold me. He would not notice, or, if he did, he would give me a quick grin that told me he too thought tonight's meal was better to play with than to eat.

I scrape my food face into the trash and wash my plate, fork, and knife in soapy water so hot my hands hurt. The pain is welcome, distracting me from the thoughts that flit behind my eyes like bats. Things I would rather not examine.

"Damn Will." Even as I say it, I know it is not his fault. He thought it was the news of Ben's cancer that subdued me. How ironic that it was his words of praise, his remark about processing my law forms. I assumed I had made the fitness certification submission deadline and had focused my worry on the exam. In Georgia, to be certified to practice law is a two-step process. You must complete a fitness certification form avowing that you are an upstanding person who pays her bills on time, has not been convicted of any felonies, and is not crazy. No, really. They ask about your mental health. I had a good chuckle about that series of questions as I filled out the form on the floor of my Manhattan apartment, surrounded by moving boxes, my life wrapped in newspaper and bubble packaging. Depressed? Unstable? Manic? Me? Of course not.

I forwarded the form to Judge Owens's address. He never told me I was months behind. Once he ascertained that I was intent on obtaining this job and that I would not be deterred by talk of long hours, low pay, relocation, and a wholly new environment, he said he would see what he could do. He did plenty, more than I knew. It seems I should have sent him a case of fine Scotch, not just a bottle.

Above the kitchen sink, the window shows my reflected outline. I look like an amorphous lump, a heavy shadow. I turn away and head for my bedroom.

When I tug the knob on my bedside table, it slides forward so fast that the drawer flies free of its grooves and lands on the floor and my feet. "Fuck!" My feet sting. I kneel on the braided rug beside my bed and look through the contents of the drawer, half of them tumbled to the rug. There it is, the picture. Me and Henry at that inn, my smile wide and stupid. How could I be so stupid?

I slam the photograph against the floor but the rug softens the blow, so I raise it higher and bring it down onto the exposed wood until I gouge its smooth varnished surface, until the glass in the frame cracks and splinters. He could have taken the blame, told his partners the mistake was his own. What would they have done? Nothing. He had to know I would not stay at the firm and file forms, that the insult would make me leave. Shards of glass slice my hand. Blood drops onto the pine-board floor, forming an uneven puddle.

I drop the photograph and cover my eyes with the heels of my hands, pressing them into my lids. Will knows about my fitness certificate. Does Ben? Is that why he resents me? Because I broke the rules to get this job? I flouted waiting periods and used my Atlanta connection to pull strings? If only he knew why. No, that would be worse.

Fucking Henry. Why? What did I demand from him but small portions of his time and heart? Tears of anger scald my cheeks. I rock back and forth on my heels. I thought he loved me. Idiot girl.

"You're such a tiger," he murmured, half jesting, after a surprise Wednesday night get-together. He traced the dip of my lower back with his index finger. His eyes were sexed up, a brighter brown than usual. "Where did you learn to do those things?"

"You," I told him, staring through lowered lashes. He knew it to be true. There was no one else. He saw the blood that first time.

"I must be one hell of a professor," he said, tugging me onto his chest.

I tear the picture through the glass, bisecting Henry's torso. I will rip it into confetti. I will destroy him. I tear it until the blood on my hands causes my fingers to slip on the shiny surface of the paper. I stare at the fragments.

I had a life, a plan, dreams, friends, parents, and I left them all. He sat in his leather chair acting as if my career and life meant nothing to him and never had. I thought that moving to Macon, taking this job, would show him, would prove I was better. Now here I am, preparing a death sentence case with a cancerous partner. I sure showed him.

My sinuses, my teeth, my chest, and my head hurt. I walk to the bathroom. My reflection is ghastly. The cuts on my hand have left bloody smears on my cheeks and underneath my nose. My eyelids are so swollen it looks as though I've suffered an allergic reaction. Mucus covers my upper lip in a clear moustache and the freckles I earned outside are invisible on my red nose. My bloody hands turn the water pink. So it begins, I think, and so it ends, with my blood. And now, as then, I cannot help but think I deserve this. My choices, all of them mine.

Chapter Sixteen

August 10, 2000

Thus far, on my drive to work, I have spotted two dead possums and a cat whose corpse bore the tread marks of enormous tires. I turn my attention from roadkill to what I will say to Ben when I see him. I picture him, thumbs hooked behind his suspenders, chest out like a robin prepared to sing. If I hold this image in my head I won't have to relive this morning: vacuuming the glass from my floor, placing the torn bits of photograph into the trash bin, wiping an overlooked blood smear from the bathroom sink. My bedroom was a crime scene.

Before I began working for the DA, I never thought about what happens to crime scenes after a crew processes them. Beyond the dusting for fingerprints and search for expelled bullets, what use could such an area have? I never considered who cleans the spilled blood of the violently murdered or who replasters walls pocked with bullets. Some people make their living sanitizing crime scenes, transforming areas where corpses once lay back into ordinary living rooms, kitchens, and bedrooms. I wonder how these people respond when asked how their day went. "Today I cleaned bits of brain from the floorboards. How was your day?"

My mind will not stay on Ben. Peripheral items keep catching my attention. I start thinking of his paunchy belly and brown tasseled leather shoes and then my gaze is caught on the white gauze mummifying my right hand. The shallow cuts were too numerous to cover with small bandages, and too noticeable not to conceal. No one will believe my story that I cut myself chopping vegetables if they see my hand.

Sure enough, the gauzy hand draws questions. It begins with George, downstairs, and continues all the way down my hall and into my office. "Potato accident," I tell Will as he slows his typical hallway dash to look at my hand. I wave him on his way with a cheerful, "Don't worry. You should see the other guy." He laughs and moves on.

In my office there is a stack of paperwork in the middle of the desk that I have no hope of clearing off by day's end. I sigh and look at the topmost sheet. A fireman's statement from the arson case. When was this delivered?

"Are you adopting my filing methods?" Ben stands inside my doorway, just as I pictured him in my head, except for the vest that replaces his suspenders. He must have a court appearance today.

I gesture to the pile. "No. Unlike your office, my office is usually pile-free."

"So I've noticed." He rocks back on his heels. I search his face for signs of illness, but see nothing in his jowly good-humored face.

"What happened to your hand?" he asks.

"Vegetable-chopping accident. Potato."

He stares at the swath of bandages. "You must have sliced yourself good." He doesn't sound displeased. "Did you go to the hospital?"

"No need. Besides, I hate hospitals, don't you?"

Ben takes a moment to answer. "No. Hospitals don't scare me."

"Oh, I'm not scared of them. I just don't like them. They smell like disenfectant and all that sterile white is hard on the eyes. Plus there are all those people, waiting for news. It's a breeding ground for anxiety."

He shuffles back a step so he is half in, half out of the doorway. "Hospitals aren't pleasant," he concedes, "but they serve their purpose." Oh ho. He is uncertain. He never would have conceded otherwise.

"I suppose." I lift my hand and look at it as if for the first time. "Perhaps I should see somebody about this. Could you recommend someone?"

"What?" He reacts as if I have just asked him for the telephone number of his cocaine dealer.

"Oh, why bother? I'm sure it will heal fast enough. I'm young and healthy." As the words leave my mouth I want to seize them back. Ben looks a little pale. I *am* young and healthy. My elation collapses with a pinprick of guilt. Whether I can see it or not, he is ill. Yes, he annoys me and baits me and disregards my politics with a shrug of distaste, but Ben has never hurt me. Although he knows Judge Owens and could hurt me if . . . if what? If he told Will I had an affair and that is the real reason I came to Macon? Will, I suspect, would not care, as long as I continued working hard.

"We will meet at two o'clock then," Ben says. He leaves after I murmur approval, unsure where I agreed to meet him. Probably his office.

Judge Owens knows that there was an incident at Walters, MacLittle, and Tate. That I was accused of making a mistake for a large client and that it was one of the partners (I refused to name which) who was responsible. Whether he investigated further or conjectured more, I do not know. It doesn't matter. I try to balance a pencil on my undamaged palm, a Lacey trick, but the pencil falls after a second. I try again.

It does not matter. Henry took advantage of me. I took advantage of Judge Owens's connections, and now here I am, turning my bandaged hand back and forth, ignoring the beep of my computer. It wants me to check my e-mails and appointments. I tune out the noise from the hall: the ring of phones and thuds of closing filing cabinets and chatter of people avoiding work for a few moments. I stare at the white gauze, thick and almost fluffy. Like the thick white marshmallow my mother put in my hot cocoa.

I consider Ben and his relationship to the judge and decide it no longer matters. Of course I never want Ben to know of my affair. God, no. But there are worse things. I place the eraser end of the pencil on my left palm and move my hand back and forth. The pencil stays upright for two seconds before it falls. Better than my previous attempts. Satisfied, I turn to my work.

I shuffle my arson paperwork to the bottom of the pile and move to the next case: the licorice thief. Helen's pleas for clemency fell on deaf ears. Not that she expected otherwise. The former Miss Georgia is talented, but you cannot strike a deal when the other party knows you have nothing to offer. After our negotiations ended with a promise to meet in court, Helen had spun around on her heels, an effortless balancing trick that spoke of her beauty pageant days. If I had attempted that maneuver in those heels I would have toppled to the floor.

"Are you going to the Georgia Trust auction next Thursday?"

I wondered how she knew.

She rested her leather-bound organizer against her hip. "It looks good if local politicos show up, but I'm betting Will tapped someone from his office to go, and since you're low man on the totem pole . . ."

Will had suggested several weeks ago that I be given the ticket the district attorney's office purchased for the auction. He had made it sound like a privilege, one I would have felt churlish refusing. Sucker.

"Is it awful?"

"No. This year it's at Hay House, to raise money for restorations. There will be food, drinks, and an auction. Last year Judge Gaverly bid six thousand dollars for a set of silk pajamas that belonged to Elvis."

I blinked. Judge Gaverly was a very large man. He was also a notorious tightfist who refused to pay his parking tickets, though he deserved every one. He treated fire hydrants like parking meters established for his exclusive use.

"I'm going. Part of my community service, penance for my job." Poor Helen. It could not be easy having a reputation as the representative of so many of Macon's least desirables.

I asked about the dress code and Helen said, "Black tie optional. I am sure you have something suitable."

I did not understand her confidence in my wardrobe. My work clothes were gray, brown, black, blue, and white, hanging stiff, as if they might shrug off the hangers and walk out of the closet. Then there were my sweatshirts, dresses, skirts, and corduroys in turquoise, magenta, purple, and black. I had never considered the dichotomy of my closet, but it appeared there were two Natalies living in my house: lawyer Natalie and playtime Natalie. Playtime Natalie needed to go shopping soon. Half of my clothes were approaching antique status, although this was less a flaw here than elsewhere. Georgians love all things old.

Before I have made it halfway through my paper pile it is two o'clock. Time to meet Ben. I gather my things and head for his office.

"Good God, it looks like Hurricane Albert hit." Papers spill onto the floor, beyond their normal lopsided piles, banker's boxes are gathered by the door, ready to trip unsuspecting visitors. His desk has one clear patch where a small piece of paper might fit. Surrounding this oasis are paper clips, rubber bands, pens, pencils, notebooks, and sticky notes. It looks as though an office supply store exploded.

Ben turns from an overstuffed closet. "Oh. Is it two? I thought we were meeting in your office."

"I can see why. It's ten past two. I was just wondering where you were." This is, of course, a lie. I had not heard him say where we were meeting.

"I'll be there in just a minute. I need to find a document for tomorrow's deposition."

"I won't hold my breath," I promise, doubting he can find anything in there "in just a minute."

He surprises me by showing up at my office two minutes later, a bottle of soda in his hand. "Found it."

"Congratulations."

He launches into pretrial talk. Jury selection is set for August 29, less than a month away. The defense's eagerness to go to trial surprised me. In their position I would have begged, borrowed, and stolen every postponement I could get. They must rate their chances for victory greater than I do. We may not have the gun, but we have a witness to Calvin Washington's confrontation with Marcus Rhodes, Calvin's fingerprints within the school, and wooden splinters, presumably from the bat used to beat Marcus, found in his car. There are blood spatters on several pieces of his clothing, consistent with Marcus's and Dominic's blood types. Calvin's hand was injured and splinters removed from it. Pieces of the bat he wielded with such power. He is guilty as hell.

Ben tells me about the chief defense counsel, Thomas Landry. "He's a sharp one. His father is a federal judge whose name was bandied about as a Supreme Court nominee in 1991 before Clarence Thomas." I fail to see how his father's consideration to the Supreme Court makes Thomas Landry a sharp one, but that just shows I'm not a Georgian. A person is defined by "their people" in Georgia, a concept that would not seem unfamiliar to a Jew who grew up outside Boston, where "your people" were a small group. However, by people, Georgians mean family, family they can trace back to William the Conqueror and beyond.

I look up because I realize the low hum of sound, of Ben talking, has stopped. He is frowning at me, the small crease line between his brows visible. It's always there, that line, but only apparent when he frowns. I bet I have seen more of that frown line than anyone.

"Sorry." It's atypical of me to apologize, but it was rude of me to stop listening and I should be paying attention and he looks a little pale. His stomach, an overfilled balloon, seems to have leaked some air. Has he lost weight? Is it the cancer, or fear of it, that has caused his pants to sit a tiny bit lower than their usual Humpty Dumpty position? Before he can continue I blurt, "Rudy Giuliani had prostate cancer."

He sighs and rubs his large hand over his face as if it is a chalkboard he is trying to erase. "Will told you."

"Yes." I hold back the "you should have."

"Look, I'm going to be fine. The doctors say so, and I don't wish to discuss my health with everyone in town."

"I am not everyone. I am your cocounsel. You should have told me, if only so that I could plan our schedules. Instead you tell me nothing, disappear for days, and get crabby when Will finally informs me what you should have told me weeks ago." So much for holding it in. "Look," I begin, ready to backtrack.

"No," he interrupts. "You're right." He stares in the direction of my earlobes. "I should have told you. I just—"

"It's okay." I wave my hand in a gesture I adopted at Walters, MacLittle, and Tate. It means "Whatever, no problem, it's fixable." I learned it from my fellow associates who used to wave away little things like missed calls from spouses and mislaid documents but who would turn tomato red with rage if a typo appeared on their embossed business cards. I hate that I still use that gesture. I have tried to quit but my hand moves independent of my will.

"Good God, Goldberg, don't you start." He withdraws a packet of peanuts from his pocket.

"Start what?" I watch as he opens the package and dumps the contents into his soda. The soda bubbles as the peanuts fall through the liquid to settle at the bottom.

"Being nice because I'm sick." He sounds fatigued. I wonder how much false sympathy he has borne, carrying the burden of other's politic politeness.

"I'm nice all the time," I tell him.

He cocks his head to one side and widens his eyes, begging for an example.

"All the time except when I'm in court or at the bargaining table or behind someone who can't make up their mind as to what flavor iced coffee they want or . . . with you."

"Uh-huh." I envy his ability to invest two syllables with more meaning than I can wrest from seventeen.

He takes a swallow of his soda. Ewwwww.

"You want to discuss our relationship some more or you want to discuss this case?" I ask.

"We don't have a relationship." He pronounces it "ree-lay-shun-ship" and it takes him five seconds to say.

"We don't?" I stop tapping my pencil against the desk.

"No, we don't."

"Darn. I guess this means I should cancel that order for matching handkerchiefs. I thought you could wear yours in your breast pocket and I could wear mine as a headband. We could be super-twins in court."

Ben stays silent. His cheek tightens. I assume he is repressing a smile because he never suppresses grimaces.

He fishes in his leather binder and withdraws a long blue envelope. "Here. This got misdirected to my office, and I opened it without looking."

Though it is addressed to me, the handwriting is shaky and difficult to read. I withdraw the card from inside.

Dear Natalie,

Thank you for the beautiful flowers. They brightened my room for over a week! Sorry for the delay, but that operation tuckered me out. I'm on the mend now, though. I shall keep you in my prayers.

Mrs. Clay Biddle

"Oh," I say. Did Ben read this? Does he wonder why I sent Mrs. Biddle flowers? I shove the note into my out box.

Ben clears his throat with two loud harrumphs. "That was nice of you, sending her flowers."

Well, that answers that question. He read the note.

"Told you I'm a softie," I say.

He harrumphs again before saying, "The defense is going to press hard on the time element."

"Why?"

"Because they have a witness who says Calvin Washington wasn't at the elementary school at six-thirty P.M." He takes another swallow of his peanut-flavored soda. I wince.

"Where does the witness say he was?"

"A gas station outside Columbus."

"What do you think?"

"The witness is wrong. Washington is our killer."

I tap my pencil against my notepad. "So we prove the witness wrong. What else?" My pulse is beating a salsa tempo in my hands. It is the rush that accompanies a new challenge.

"We need to look into the murder weapon. It's gone, but I would like to document Washington's relationship to guns. Prior ownership."

"You know I have a hard time imagining our Founding Fathers meant to include semiautomatic handguns under the Second Amendment." I speak from long-established habit, taking up the handgun-control flag and waving it whenever possible.

Ben, a card-carrying NRA member, grunts and says, "So I'll assume you would like to tackle that project. Be sure to spread the word among the gun dealers you encounter."

Ugh. Gun dealers. "I will," I promise. "You think I should bring some petitions for them to sign?" I contort my face into my best dumb-girl expression. He just shakes his head. My own cheek tightens with a repressed smile.

"What does that taste like?" I gesture toward his drink. I cannot resist asking.

"This?" he says. "Soda and peanuts? A true Southern treat.

They say Jimmy Carter drank this. He was a peanut farmer from Georgia."

"I know. He was also a Democrat."

"Nobody's perfect," Ben says before taking another swig.

"Ugh," I say, causing him to smile.

We're back, just like before.

Chapter Seventeen

August 13, 2000

I lean my elbows onto the kitchen tabletop and reach for the stack of bills awaiting payment. I write out a check for Georgia Power Company. On the portion of the bill I retain, I note how much I paid, with which number check, and on what date. The same information goes into my checkbook. I file the bills, alphabetically, into an accordion folder. Check number #1131 for $58.04 paid on August 13, 2000. I put the bill receipt and check into the envelope, lick the gummy seal and run my finger against the surface, hard. I use standard U.S. flag stamps, because it seems silly to send stamps with hearts or Elvis faces. The same way it has always seemed absurd to buy personalized checks with animals or sports logos on them. Why would you want to make the act of payment a warm and fuzzy one?

As I flip the register page over in my checkbook I see a note for "Rose Factory" dated June 11. My mother's birthday gift, sent three days late. I procrastinated about choosing a gift and then sent her roses. Cliché at best, but I could not intuit anything she needed or even wanted, except for me to move back to Cambridge. So I sent a birthday bouquet of pink roses. She called to say thank you the next day. It was an awkward conversation, made more so by the fact that I could hear my father in the background. He refused to come to the phone, pleading he would talk to me "another time."

I scan the pages of my checkbook register. There is a lot of activity in the summer of 1999. There are the checks to the movers, rent checks, checks for new furniture, towels, and dishes, a new life. I frown at a few entries. "BBQ Barn" where I got my first real taste of anti-Yankee sentiment. The manager tried to refuse my check, but the restaurant didn't take American Express and I had three dollars on me. He stared at my all-black outfit and muttered something about cheap Northerners.

Another check paid for "Temple Beth Shalom," my family's synagogue. Despite the fact I live hundred of miles away and thus cannot attend services, I still send money for membership. My ticket for the High Holiday admission gets filed in a small, jeweled box my mother gave me years ago. I cannot bring myself to throw the tickets out. It feels sacrilegious. Adultery and lying I can do but temple ticket disposal, no. Idiocy, thy name is Natalie Ruth Goldberg.

A swallow of coffee laced with brandy sears my chest. I raise my cup in silent tribute to Lala, who introduced me to this after-dinner drink. She credits her good health to it, and claims that her mother and grandmother supported its medicinal qualities. I take another hit and smile. Medicine, indeed.

I wonder if Ben is taking any medicines. The *Merck Manual* sits on my bookshelf, ready to be consulted. I had planned to look up prostate cancer, to understand what it attacks, how it can be treated, but I have not opened the book yet. Is it fear that keeps me from looking? Or an unwillingness to concentrate my attention on what is happening inside Ben's body?

The last dregs of coffee and brandy impart fleeting warmth. I pick up my pen to write the remainder of the checks. Rent, gas, cable television, credit card, my subscription to *The National Law Journal*, telephone, and car insurance. I cannot help the smile from tugging at my lips. Macon may be many things, but expensive it is not. After paying twice as much in rent for a one-bedroom apartment in Manhattan, my monthly rent for a two-bedroom house seems ludicrous. I chew my lip, recalling the conversation I had with my landlady last month. She asked if I would consider buying the house.

Mrs. Miller, widowed with three children, lives with her oldest daughter in Milledgeville, a few towns over. She is a sweet lady with a shell of white hair lacquered harder than any helmet. She lived in this house with her husband after he retired from his job as a civil engineer with the department of public works. They lived here four years before he died. After that, she moved in with her daughter and began renting the place out. I was delighted to find something so spacious and so close to work, but the idea of owning it, of buying property in Macon, knocked the breath from me. When Mrs. Miller telephoned to ask if I might wish to buy it I had dithered, saying I would consider it.

I rub the raised hand-stenciled ivy print on the table with my fingers and consider her offer. The house is forty years old and well maintained. The neighborhood is safe. The school attached to this district is excellent. What am I thinking? I am not raising a family here, for God's sake. I don't even own a cat. I gather the paid bills and settle them into a neat pile. I put the stamps in the kitchen basket that holds odds and ends: pens, paper clips, tape, and scissors. I touch the woven wood of the basket, my eyes focused on the pale blue wall behind it. The paints in this place are perfect. Yellow in the living room, pale blue in the kitchen, cream in the bedroom with just a touch of peach. Soft colors, nothing loud and no anonymous white. It's a nice house with lots of closets.

The accordion folder of bills gets returned to the "sewing room" as Mrs. Miller calls it. I transformed it into my personal office and library. Beside a small two-drawer desk stands a bookcase filled with legal reference books, a few dictionaries, fiction paperbacks, and established literary tomes from college. My gaze falls to a volume wedged between *Corporation Law* and the *The Chicago Manual of Style. Righting Wrongs: Important Cases in American Civil Liberties*, edited by Aaron Goldberg. It was published when I was twelve. I made him sign my copy. He wrote: *To my daughter Natalie, future people's champion. With much love from your father.* I stare at the book and breathe in and out, listening for something, anything. Nothing happens. I turn away and close the door.

Chapter Eighteen

August 17, 2000

Tonight the open windows and doors of Hay House are just adequate to cool the people circulating through the expansive downstairs rooms. Constructed in the 1850s, Hay House is known for its early "air-conditioning" ventilation system and central heating, conveniences unheard of in houses of that period. Of course, most houses of the period didn't cost a hundred thousand dollars or have five-hundred-pound wooden front doors painted to resemble metal. These are some of the features that make Hay House special, and compel people to bid on auctioned items tonight. That is the declared purpose anyway: to restore the house. I suspect people came to socialize, to see and be seen, and because there is an excitement about auctions, the element of surprise.

According to Mrs. Mary Hale, director of the central library in Macon, one of the surprises is the donation of a painting by an unidentified celebrity. Once the final bid is accepted, the winner will be informed of the artist's identity. Mrs. Hale informs me, between delicate bites of sliced fruit, that she does not know the identity of the painter, but she does know that the painter is famous for another type of art.

"Movies?" I ask.

"Perhaps. People are wild for movie stars nowadays."

I adore how she makes this seem a modern concept.

Mrs. Hale has shed her usual plaid suit for a vivid peach dress with matching handbag. Women in pinks, fuchsias, and yellows surround me.

"Nice outfit," Helen says, tapping my right shoulder. I smile hello, relieved by her arrival. "Very New York." She nods a greeting to Mrs. Hale who returns the nod.

My dress is a black knee-length silk sheath. "My friend Lacey calls black 'urban camouflage,' " I tell her.

She fingers my hand-dyed purple and red scarf. "Beautiful. Where did you get it?"

"Lacey gave it to me. Birthday present." The scarf makes anything look chic.

"Well, you won't blend in, at any rate." Helen surveys the crowd. She looks over most heads in the room. In heels, she is six feet tall. "Oh, my," she murmurs. "Oh, my. Have you seen Mrs. McKinney?"

"Mrs. McKinney?" The name sounds familiar but I can't recall why.

"Town council member, headed for the fruit tray. Just wait." Helen watches me watch Mrs. McKinney approach the mango and pineapple. I do not understand Helen's interest. Mrs. McKinney looks of average height and medium build and middle age. She turns to spear a slice of watermelon and I gasp. Mrs. McKinney's dress descends into a vee that ends near her waist.

"Who ordered the mutton dressed as lamb?" Helen murmurs. A snort of laughter escapes me.

"Let's grab a drink and some canapés before they disappear."

She grabs my wrist and tugs me forward. "I haven't eaten all day." I follow her through the marble hall and into the next room where three bartenders stand behind a table. One of them is white, which amuses me. The majority of attendees are black, reflecting the makeup of Macon. The last U.S. Census put the ratio at 63 percent African American and 35 percent white. I have grown used to being outnumbered, but in this room, with so many bare-shouldered women, I do feel conspicuously pale.

Helen, paler than me, with her beacon of blond hair, seems not to notice. She is busy getting a mint julep and signaling one of the servers to bring the hors d'oeuvres tray to her. Delighted to be the object of her attention, he hurries forward and stumbles over the foot of a man who stands talking with two other men. The server recovers, and neither of the men, dressed in dark suits and bow ties, says anything. Helen unloads four treats from the silver tray onto a small plate. I take a miniature asparagus tart. Helen warns the server "not to go far" in a voice that threatens violence. Three minutes later, her appetizers are gone.

"You really didn't eat, did you?" I ask.

"Nope," she says, rolling her eyes toward the stenciled ceiling. The gesture, combined with her loose hair, makes her look much younger. "I was in court until four, and then I got a call from a client who had just been picked up on charges of assaulting his brother-in-law." Carl's face flashes in my mind, although I know it can't be him. He is in Bermuda now, sipping a frothy drink and watching the ocean waves crash onto shore. "Thank God I had my dress with me. I showered and changed at the office and came straight here."

"Your office has a shower?"

"Uh-huh. It gets a lot of use." She approaches the server who remained close by. Helen relieves his silver platter of two more crab puffs.

"So you're in it for the glamour, then?" I ask.

"Huh?"

"Law. I assume there's a reason you chose it."

"You're such a Yankee." She softens the comment with a smile. "Most people down here just say, 'So what's a pretty girl like you doing working?' "

"I think women should work—"

"Super-Yankee," she interrupts.

"I just wondered why you chose law."

"Over, say, modeling?"

She seems determined to find insults in my questions.

"I tried it. I even moved to New York City." She grimaces, causing tiny lines to fan from her eyes. "I lasted seven months. All that noise, all those people, all those rules. Don't eat this. Don't eat that. Don't eat, period."

She swallows the last of her crab puffs. I can see where the no-eating rule would disagree with her.

"I hated it, so I came home. Went to UGA. Then my father got busted for burglary and that's when I decided to become a lawyer. So the next time my dad ended up in the pokey we wouldn't have to spend the mortgage payment on lawyer's fees."

"Your father was convicted of burglary?" My voice squeaks. I am stunned.

"Several. Car theft, burglary, manslaughter. You hadn't heard? I thought for sure your pals at the DA would have told you all about the daughter of Jimmy Two Times."

"Jimmy Two Times?"

"That was his nickname. My father. He used to have this habit of rapping the table two times when he had a great poker hand. He was an awful card player. You really hadn't heard?"

"No." It surprises me that such choice gossip should have escaped my ears. While nice to believe professional respect curbed my colleagues' tongues, it is unlikely. More believable is that people expected I had heard the tale from someone else.

"I did hear all about your Miss Georgia victory, though."

"The stories of my triumph are exaggerated," she drawls, batting her eyelashes.

A soft tap on my shoulder interrupts our conversation.

"Excuse me," a soft voice apologizes. I pivot to find a black couple standing before me. I know the woman. Dominic's mother. She wears a black dress and looks much older than the last time I saw her. Deep ruts are carved around her mouth. The man beside her holds her elbow and must be her husband. He stands a foot taller, wearing a deep gray suit and white dress shirt that matches the white patches of hair at his temples.

"Yes?"

"Are you Natalie Goldberg?" she asks.

"Yes."

"From the DA's office?" She is uncertain, as if there is a pack of Goldbergs running about Macon.

I nod. "I thought so," she says, half to her husband, half to herself. "I'm Emily Brown, and this is my husband, Douglas."

What to say? I know who you are. I am terribly sorry for your loss.

"Miss Goldberg," he says, his voice deep and smooth, like syrup. "I believe you are handling our son's case."

"Yes, I am. The chief counsel is my colleague Ben Maddox. Do you know him?" The Browns shake their heads. I look about the room as if Ben will appear. "He's not here." I lower my voice. "I am very sorry for your loss."

"We just wanted to say thank you," Emily says, reaching forward to grasp my hand. Her skin is dry and cool, too cool, as if her blood has ceased circulating.

"I met you once," The words spill out of me, in a rush. "You and your son. At the Piggly Wiggly."

She puzzles over this. I say, "He was practicing his magic."

"Oh!" she murmurs. "Oh yes. Yes." Tears gather at the corners of her eyes.

"We know you will see that our boy's murderer is brought to justice," her husband says. "'For whoso sheddeth man's blood, by man shall his blood be shed: for in the image of God made he man.' " He is a Baptist minister. That was in the report.

I cannot bear to look at his eyes, bright with grief and vengeance. What can I say to this couple, aged prematurely by grief? "I'll do my best."

Douglas squeezes his wife's elbow and she grips my hand again, cutting the blood flow to my fingers. "We'll keep you in our prayers," she promises. They leave, heading for the hall.

"Oh, my," Helen murmurs, arching her shaped brows at me. "I hadn't thought they would come tonight."

I monitor their progress through the house. People are keeping their distance, as if the Browns are contagious.

"They are active with local preservation causes. He is on the board of directors of the Tubman House. They haven't been out much since Dominic died."

I sigh, aware that people are watching me. Their eyes feel like fingers, tickling my neck and shoulders. I shrug, as if I can dislodge their attention.

"You okay?" Helen asks.

"I could use a drink." I head for the bartenders and the promise of an antidote.

We collect our drinks—another mint julep for Helen and a gin and tonic for me—and head for the music room where the auction is to be held.

Wooden folding chairs stand in ten rows, with a small aisle in between. It looks like preparations for a wedding ceremony, except that at the front of the white and gold wallpapered room, instead of an altar, is a podium and table. To the left stands an empty easel.

"Wonder what the subject is?" Helen asks, pointing toward the easel with her auction paddle, which resembles a wooden Ping-Pong paddle. Hers has 41 painted in black on it. Mine has 18, colored red.

"Impressionist landscape?" I say.

"I'm guessing nude self-portrait."

I am saved from pointing out that a self-portrait would make the identity of the painter less than secret by the thunk-thunk of the gavel against the podium. Mayor Barry Sims stands at the podium, dressed in a pin-striped suit. His wide face, always smiling, reminds me of a black Santa.

"Good evening, ladies and gentlemen, and thank you for coming to Hay House tonight. As you know, we Maconians love this structure, not only because it's beautiful but because it brings us tourist dollars." A titter of laughter ripples outward across the room. "And tonight we hope to raise funds to ensure that this historic home will be enjoyed by future generations of visitors. So, please enjoy yourself and overbid!"

Another small wave of laughter breaks. I survey the rows of chairs before me. I do not see the dark-clad figures of the Browns. Perhaps they did not stay for the auction. The idea that they came to see me makes me tug at my dress hem.

The event organizers have hired a real auctioneer, one of those men who warble words into guttural strings of sounds. It's hard to follow, so I simply watch the paddles go up and down, up and down, like horses on a carousel. When a set of pig bookends is set at the table up front I giggle, but the noise goes unnoticed. Women sit straighter in their chairs and a buzz of low whispers fills the room, like static from a badly tuned radio. Helen leans toward me to say, "They're Carlton Ware." I assume she is referring to the pigs.

The auctioneer announces the merchandise. "A pristine set of Carlton Ware pink pig bookends." I let another giggle escape. I cannot help it. The little pig, bisected in half by a maroon volume used to display the purpose of the bookends, is too funny.

This little piggy went to auction, I think.

I am amazed to hear the bidding open at twenty-five dollars, and am further astonished when half of the paddles in the room are raised, like the hands of overachieving schoolchildren. Helen raises her paddle twice, but drops out when the bidding reaches sixty dollars. My jaw lowers as the caller says, "Ninety, ma'am, ninety, thank you, ninety-five?" It feels like I have run a race when he calls out, "One hundred thirty-five, sold to Mrs. Francis, for one hundred thirty-five." I exhale in a rush of breath.

"What was all the fuss for?" I demand of Helen, who is applauding for tiny Mrs. Francis, whose shiny cocoa face beams with delight at having won her prize. Her husband, seated beside her, looks nonplussed.

"Carlton Ware is very popular. The company went out of business in the eighties, but their stuff's value has gone through the roof. Have you ever seen their eggcups with the little feet at the bottom?"

I think she must be pulling my leg, playing some sort of pin-the-joke-on-the-Yankee.

"Guess not," she says and I realize she is serious. Eggcups with feet. How bizarre.

The auctioneer pulls a small jewelry box from behind the piggy bookends. "Ladies and gentlemen, for lovers of fine jewelry we have a beautiful one-carat ruby ring set in eighteen-karat filigree. This item was available for examination during the prebid show. A beautiful ring, fit for a queen. Let us start the bidding at fifty dollars. Do

I have fifty dollars? Fifty dollars? Fifty dollars here, thank you. Sixty dollars, yes, thank you."

My eyes never waver from the box holding the ring. I remember the small scar Henry had at his temple from where a horse kicked him. He quit smoking two years before we met. His hair felt softer than it looked. He did not enjoy the movies. He was left-handed and allergic to strawberries.

The ruby looks small from my seat, but I know it is big enough to reach my knuckle. Henry liked knock-knock jokes. His right foot was bigger than his left.

"Two hundred and fifty dollars." He loved animals, especially horses, despite his near-death encounter. His favorite season was winter. He sang off-key. He preferred his shirts starched.

"Three hundred dollars." He liked to give presents more than he liked receiving them. He said "gesundheit" when he heard someone sneeze. He called me Lee when we were together.

"Three hundred and seventy-five dollars. Sold!" The gavel closes the bidding. It is over, at last.

I shift in my seat and look about the room. Mrs. McKinney's cleavage is drawing stares. Helen notices. "Perhaps she is planning to offer them up to the highest bidder. I hear her marriage is on the skids."

"That's awful," I chastise, smoothing the hem of my dress.

"Speaking of people in the market, how's the office hunk?" she asks, causing me to squint at her. Is she drunk?

"Huh? What office hunk?" I blow a stray curl off my brow using a short blast of breath from the corner of my mouth.

"Carl Andrews."

"You know Carl?"

"Not as well as I'd like to know him. He's the type I wouldn't kick out of bed for eating crackers."

"Yeah, and he has more tics than a dirty dog in summer," I say. I cover my mouth, a guilt reflex.

"Nerves? I've never noticed. He always seems calm in court."

I shrug. I have seen Carl in court just once. He prosecutes the sex crimes, and I try to stay away from those cases.

"He's a good guy," I add, feeling bad for my prior comment.

Helen looks about the room. "Not many of them around these days."

"That good, huh?"

"Even worse," she answers. "Oh!" She grabs my arm. "I think they're bringing in the painting now!"

Everyone in the room has turned to look at the rear doors through which we entered. Two men carry a large rectangle covered in blue velvet. As they walk down the aisle I resist the urge to hum the "Wedding March." Instead, I watch people stir. The auctioneer carefully settles the painting on the easel. The cacophony dies to a few whispers, loud in the near silence. When all noise has been vacuumed from the room, the auctioneer casts aside the fabric to reveal a series of lines and circles, painted in bright primary colors upon a blank canvas. The room appears to be holding its breath. Whatever we were expecting, it wasn't a third-rate Pollock study.

I worry that Macon's celebrity donation isn't going to pay off, not like Elvis's pajamas. But several paddles go up when the bidding begins at one thousand dollars.

"It's hideous," Helen says. "My five-year-old niece can do better!"

"Yes, but is she a celebrity?" I ask, as the bidding rises to thirty-five hundred dollars. The two fiercest competitors are Miss Wilcox, who made a fortune marketing cosmetics for African Americans in the 1960s, and a white man I don't recognize.

"Who's that?" I ask, pointing my paddle toward the goateed bidder.

"Gregory Hurcombe, a real estate mogul in Atlanta. His parents are from Macon. He likes to throw money around for good causes. Makes him feel important." The venom in her tone makes me wonder how she knows him, but I don't ask, too busy watching Miss Wilcox's paddle rise in opposition to Mr. Hurcombe's.

"Sold to Mr. Hurcombe for fifteen thousand dollars."

Chump change considering it's a celebrity-created work of art, but a fortune when one takes a close look at said art. I hope Hurcombe considers it worth the money when he finds out who painted it. I set my paddle on the now empty chair beside me and rise. My legs are stiff. I need to get to bed.

People are beginning to clear the room, some muttering comments about the "terrible painting." These people know bad art when they see it.

Helen yawns, belatedly raising her hand to cover her mouth. I half expect her to rub her eyes, as overtired children do. Instead she tucks a strand of blond hair behind her ear with unstudied grace.

"Are you parked outside?" she asks. I nod.

"Me, too. I'll walk with you."

We exit the room, following in the wake of the crowd before us. It seems the event was a success. I overhear the auction's total estimated at $53,000. This will go toward refinishing the house's two-story octagonal cupola. Once we are far enough away from the house to view it from the drive, I look at the cupola's gleaming white exterior. It stands high above the surrounding trees, magnolias, and cedars that date back to the nineteenth century.

"It really is lovely," I murmur.

"I used to hate touring this place as a kid," Helen confesses. Our feet crunch on the gravel. "I had read some Nancy Drew mystery set in a mansion that scared the bejesus out of me, and I pictured Hay House when I read it. So having to go upstairs and look into the rooms was awful." She laughs. "Pretty silly now, but it seemed terrible at the time."

"I can imagine. Nancy Drew used to scare me, too." I pause beside a clump of flowers bordering the path. The deep red of their roselike petals glows even in the pale light. "I wonder what these are?"

"Confederate rose. *Hibiscus mutabilis*," she says.

I wonder why I bother to ask, "Are you a gardener?"

"Claimed the Macon Fair's blue ribbon for lilies two years in a row," she singsongs.

"I'm just learning. My neighbor, Lala, has been teaching me all about plants and flowers."

"Lala Dayton? I know her! She always has beautiful cuttings at the garden swap."

"The garden behind her house is gorgeous. It smells like heaven."

"Good God, I hope no one overhears us talking flowers," she says, looking over her shoulder for potential eavesdroppers. "It's bad enough we're female. No reason to load the gun for them." "Them" are men, and I know what she means.

"Oh, my gun's been loaded with the safety off since I got here. A Goldberg from Boston."

"You never had a chance," she agrees. We stop beside a silver Honda. "This is me," she says. I expected a flashier car, something more Miss Georgia.

"I had a good time." I feel silly, making end-of-the-night date sounds.

"Me, too, Nat. Maybe we can get together and talk garden shop sometime."

"I'd like that," I say, and I would. Even more, I like that she called me Nat.

Driving home I realize that I have forgotten who won the auction for the ruby ring. I wish that person better luck with it than I had.

Chapter Nineteen

August 23, 2000

"You don't find it strange?" I am incredulous, not only at Ben's position but at his mulish refusal to see it my way.

"No."

"Wait. You don't think that it is at all arbitrary?"

"What are you getting at, Goldberg?"

"What I'm getting at is how warped it is. I mean, the Georgia General Assembly voted to change the death penalty from the electric chair to lethal injection, but instead of saying everyone on death row dies by needle they say only those who are convicted of a capital crime that they committed *after* May first get the needle. For everyone else it's the chair, including Mr. Calvin Washington. There is no choice involved."

"Prisoners aren't usually given a choice."

"But it's absurd to have two systems! One which is perceived as more humane, although I'm not sure it is, and the other which some argue is barbaric and violates Fourteenth Amendment rights. I don't favor either, but why not choose one?"

Ben swallows a bite of his sandwich and levels me with a look. It is supposed to shut me up. After a few moments he sighs, rubs his face, and says, "Some members of the assembly were arguing for the change because they knew the electric chair might be ruled unconstitutional in the future, and they wanted to safeguard the death penalty by adopting lethal injection. Those same people might not have felt it was a better option."

He is honest. "It's still nuts," I say.

"Goldberg, we are working on a case, right?"

"Right." I look at my watch. Nine-thirty P.M. Most people have been home for hours.

"How did the gun dealers work out?" Ben asks.

"Go fish," I tell him.

"Pardon?"

"I found one guy who identified Washington as a potential customer, but he didn't give me anything better than that he had seen him before and that Washington never bought anything. Too cheap, he said."

"We'll forget the gun, then. The defense will make a fuss, but if we appear to take it as seriously as they do then it looks bad that we can't find it."

"We have the baseball splinters," I remind him. Plus blood-type matches of the victims on Washington's clothes. He claims it's his friend's blood, the result of a kitchen mishap. I will enjoy watching the defense try to sell that story.

He takes another bite of his sandwich. The tofu special I got delivered is pathetic next to Ben's toasted bread smeared with mayonnaise and heaped with bright red tomatoes, lettuce, and wonderful-smelling bacon. I really wanted a roast beef sandwich but I thought watching his face react to my tofu would be even better. My stomach disagrees.

Ben wipes his mouth with a thin paper napkin and I marvel at how awful he looks. His face is covered by mossy stubble, half blond, half gray, that looks on the soft side of fuzzy. There are small bald spots where it appears no hair can grow near his jawline. Not like my father, who awakens with a new forest of black facial hair each morning and who shaves twice a day while appearing in court.

I try to forget my father and concentrate on Ben's lips, which are moving. No sound seems to be issuing from them. We are an absurd sleep-deprived pair. Unshaven, gray-faced Ben murmuring, and slow-minded zombie me unable to make my ears work. Dumb and dumber.

"Has anyone ever told you that you look like the sheriff from *In the Heat of the Night*?" I ask. Why pretend I heard a word he said?

"Yes."

"Oh." I decide to return to talking trial, as he seems uninterested in my opinion of his appearance. "I think we should break the possible alibi last." I have wanted to run this by him, though I am sure he will find a way to discredit my idea.

"Why not first?" Just as I expected.

"The alibi is the defense's best hope. We have piles of physical evidence, but if they can make the jurors believe that Washington couldn't have been at the school at the time of the murders then they have won reasonable doubt. I think we should leave it alone, until the end. When we show them it's no good, it will erase any doubt in the jurors' heads. To them, it will seem all over. By that point the defense will have nothing to counter with."

I rub grit from my eyes. It sounds good. I try to envision what the defense will think when we don't push back hard on the time element early on. Will they think we are indifferent, lazy, or stupid? Hell, let them think all three. Playing dumb can be a great strategy.

"Okay," Ben says. "You take on Abraham Gentry."

"Me?"

"You want to do it this way, you take on the man giving the alibi."

I am stunned and terrified. Abraham Gentry is a key witness for the defense. I had not expected to cross-examine any witnesses. "Are you sure?" I want to kick myself for asking.

"Yes. Just one thing."

"Yes?"

"Don't screw it up." His eyes bore into mine and I realize that failing before Ben would be worse than losing this case.

"Does that stuff taste like anything?" He gestures toward my tofu. It sits in a bed of wilted greens, covered in a sauce that contains MSG and little else.

"Not really," I admit.

"Carl was eating some the other day." He makes it sound as if there is a tofu epidemic in the office and fears he may be its next victim.

"Carl looks good. Very tan, very relaxed," I say. Carl returned to the office two days ago from his Bermuda vacation, his teeth blindingly white against his darker skin.

"Lucky bastard," Ben grumbles and I smile. We have all told Carl how good he looks and how happy we are to see him and we are all thinking "lucky bastard" in our heads. Leave it to Ben to say it.

"I just got his postcard yesterday. Why is it postcards arrive after people have returned from their vacations?" I ask.

"*You* got a postcard?" It seems Ben didn't. I try to keep from blushing, and fail.

He stares at me for a moment before saying, "Postcards take so long because all the mailmen read them." Funny, but Lacey says the very same thing.

"We only have one copy of the Gentry testimony," he says, rooting around in one of his many legal boxes marked WASHINGTON in bold black letters. He hands me a bound sheaf of papers with Abraham Gentry's name on top. "Why don't you make a copy for yourself?"

It is ten o'clock at night and there are no secretaries or interns about to photocopy, but I still can't help saying, "*Darf min gehn in kolledj?*"

"What?" he says.

I don't bother to translate my Yiddish complaint of "For this I went to college?" for him. Why is it I only speak Yiddish around Ben? Maybe because all my favorite phrases involve complaints or laments and he evokes them all.

The copy machine hums and groans after I punch its buttons. This machine looks older than I am, and is nothing like the high-tech gadgets of my former Manhattan office. Will once joked that the difference between public and corporate law was the difference between a piggy bank and a chain of national banks.

I refill my paper cup of water from the cooler, noting that once again I have managed to eke the last cup out. I never change the water bottles. They are too heavy.

When I return to his office Ben's eyes are closed and a soft snuffling issues from his open lips. I think about leaving, returning to my office, and letting him sleep. I could put his coat over him. I hesitate. He breathes a bit louder, more of a snort. I hold the sheaf of papers two feet above his desk and let them drop. Bang! Ben's head jerks, his eyes roll about, and he yells, "What? What?" One of these days I will grow up, but not today.

"Here are your originals," I say, and smile.

"Oh, right." He reaches for them, squints at them as if he has forgotten what they are, and then returns them to the box behind his desk.

"Where were we?"

"You were sleeping while I was doing grunt work."

"You call that grunt work?" He sits up in his chair and points a pen in the direction of his door. "When I first got here, I was fresh out of college. Guvnor used to call me into his office every morning. He would sit at his giant desk and stare at his fingernails. He was the only man I knew who had manicures. Apparently he played the piano and liked for his hands to always look good." Ben squints at the door, seeing something I cannot, as it is in his past.

"Anyway, Guvnor used to ask me a question every day. Law questions. Sometimes criminal, often not. If I got it wrong he would send me out to tell Sally, his secretary, to fetch him a cup of coffee. If I got it right, the coffee order was canceled or he would call Sally himself."

"So Sally knew whether you got the question right or wrong."

"Yes, and she would tell the whole office. I later learned there was a betting pool, with a calendar. People chose days and placed bets on whether I would get it right or wrong."

I try to imagine Ben, younger, sweating it out in front of what is now my desk, aware that if he answered incorrectly the whole office would know and some would even profit from it.

"After a while I realized Guvnor's questions were related to my current cases. In some ways, he was helping me, making me think of topics and precedents I would have overlooked if he had not quizzed me on them."

"So you enjoyed it?"

He rolls his eyes. "I hated it. But I learned a lot."

Sort of like working with you? I don't say it, but I think it, and I suspect he knows.

"I suppose we should call it a night. You have the Gentry papers. Study them in the next few days."

"Okay." I hide a yawn behind my hand.

He throws away his dinner remains, bits of potato chips and lettuce pieces that escaped his sandwich. I watch, almost too tired to rise. Pieces of paper napkin and chips miss the rim of his wastebasket. The cleaning staff must love him.

He knocks over a picture and I pick it up. An older man wearing a fedora, carrying a big gun, with a dead tiger slung over his shoulder. Yikes.

"My grandfather." He takes the photo and puts it back. "He liked to hunt big game. Shot six rhinos and an elephant."

My nose crinkles in automatic disgust. Then I remember something guaranteed to top that tale. "My maternal grandfather was a mohel."

"A what?"

"A mohel. The Jewish doctor who performs the bris milah." I give him a second to guess, then explain, "Circumcision. I think he must have bagged himself about a thousand foreskins."

My nose wrinkle was nothing compared to his openmouthed horror.

I gather my notebook, papers, pen, and empty paper cup. I cross the threshold when Ben calls, "Goldberg."

"Yes?"

"Give me a sec to get my things and I will escort you."

It is late and the building is deserted. Our security guard left hours ago. "Okay," I agree. "Just let me fetch my briefcase."

Ben is waiting at the elevator when I emerge from my office with my briefcase, which contains the Gentry papers. I should not stay up to read them but I doubt I will be able to resist. My first cross-examination of a capital murder trial witness. I want to know as much as I can, now.

Inside the elevator I say, "I met him once."

Ben frowns and the wrinkle appears in his forehead. "Who?"

"Dominic Brown." I lean my back against the rear wall and sigh. "In the Piggly Wiggly. He was pocketing some bubble gum. I assumed he was trying to shoplift but he told his mother he was practicing his magic trick."

The elevator shudders, then stops, and after a half-minute, opens its door with a shriek of grinding metal. Ben winces.

"I was working out his sentence, assuming he was a thief. I had a lot of thefts that week."

"Don't say anything you wouldn't repeat in court," he says, opening the front door for me. "Could you prove it was theft?"

My car looks smaller in the dark, a hunched metal turtle. "No."

"Then let's assume it was a magic trick." His gaze is directed up, above the streetlights toward the three-quarter moon.

"Yes, let's," I say. My chest loosens, and I realize that since I recognized his face in those crime scene photos, I have wanted to believe in magic. Why sully a dead child's name?

Ben walks me to my car door. In the moonlight he looks, for the very first time, like a man who has battled cancer.

"Good night, Ben," I say.

He waves at me after I close my door and then shuffles off to his own car parked a hundred feet away. I cannot see it from here, but affixed to the back of his sedan is a sticker that reads, "Ted Kennedy's car has killed more people than my gun." He is a funny guy, that Ben.

Chapter Twenty

August 29, 2000

There is a fly somewhere in the courtroom. I try to ignore the insect's buzzing and concentrate on the group sitting in the jury box, waiting. Day one of voir dire, jury selection, for *State of Georgia* v. *Washington.* I look past the shoulder of potential juror number one, at a white water stain caused by a plumbing leak in the early nineties. Before my time, but the stain is familiar. I've stared at it often enough.

We lucked out, getting to play on our home court. The defense could have pushed for a change of venue, during the appeals hearing, but Ben said Landry omitted it from his eight-page list of points for redress. The gamble would have been successful with heavy press coverage of the murders, but publicity about the crimes and victims has been sparse. It seems people are less intrigued by school shootings if the shooters were not students themselves. The nation's focus is on Columbine and the mini-Columbines that followed, one in Savannah in March.

The assembled jurors look about the courtroom, many of them

seeing it from this vantage point for the first time. Does it add to the symbol of power, this elevation? Or are they hoping to answer a question wrong, so that they can drive away from the courthouse and the trial and the prospect of judging another person's right to live? Ben waits beside me in silence. That damned fly is still buzzing about.

Judge Herbert Pullman sits in the most elevated seat, scowling down at all below him with flint-colored eyes. He is not angry. That scowl is his default expression. I saw him smile once and the stretching of those thin lips to reveal pale pink gums and crooked teeth is among the top ten scariest things I have ever seen. Judge Pullman is reputed to be fair, a moderate in a judicial pool full of extremists. His scowl deepens before he clears his throat and addresses the jury box.

"Ladies and gentlemen, welcome to the Bibb County courthouse. Some of you may be new to the process of jury selection, and for those of you who are not, I would recommend you pay strict attention since this case is a little different from others you may have served on. The case you are being considered for as jurors, *State* v. *Washington*, is a capital case, meaning that the defendant faces the death penalty if found guilty of the crimes he is to stand trial for." He leans forward, encompassing all the jurors in his unblinking gaze. They stare, obedient schoolchildren, ready to digest their lesson.

"Now you remember those juror questionnaires you filled out? Well, the district attorney"—Judge Pullman nods to Ben and me—"and the defense"—a head bob in Thomas Landry's direction—"are going to ask you some questions based on your answers, and some new questions. So please answer honestly. If, after this, you are asked to leave, you are excused from jury duty and we thank you for your time. It is not a reflection on your character." I repress a smile. Judge Pullman's "character" is a mountainous adjective that slopes up and down and up again. First syllable up, second syllable down, third syllable up.

"The district attorney's office will begin." He nods again to Ben, who rises from his chair, pushing it back with a loud screech that startles the people in the jury box, awakening them from their torpor. Assessing their alert faces, I wonder if he scraped the chair on purpose.

He coughs, eyes the assembled group, and smiles. The smile reminds one of a kind uncle. It is cheerful and inviting and says, "Hey, we're pals, right?" I have seen its effect on others, witnessed the relaxed shoulders and returned smiles it causes, never having experienced that smile myself. No, for me it is always the middle-of-the-eyes frown.

Ben says, "First, let me thank you for coming this morning. We appreciate your willingness to serve as jurors. It is an important duty, and a grave responsibility. And one hell of an inconvenience when you have a pile of work to complete or children who need minding, am I right?" The people laugh and nod. I expect the judge to call Ben out for his expenditure of time making friends, but he doesn't.

"Now, I'll begin by asking each of you some questions. Mr. Dillard?"

The man in the back row, wearing a red and blue plaid shirt, looks up as if startled to hear his name. "Yes, sir?"

"Now, Mr. Dillard, you're still a resident of Payne?"

"Yes, sir."

I scribble "respectful" next to his name. My job today: psychological profiler. I have to study each juror, mark their habits, responses, and any impressions I have. We will use this information when we make our strikes, dismissing those jurors without cause we do not want. We have ten strikes. The defense has twenty. It is supposed to level the playing field. We go first.

"And you work at Grainger?"

Mr. Dillard nods. "Yes, sir. I am a salesperson for Grainger."

"And you've been there how long?"

"Four years. Before that I worked for Seelig Furniture, before they went out of business."

Ben nods, as if he is familiar with the business of layoffs. "Mr. Dillard, you have two children?"

A parent could be good for us. No one wants to see a little boy's corpse, but a parent might want to see it even less and want retribution even more. "Yes, sir. A boy and a girl, Kevin and Leila. Kevin's thirteen and Leila's ten."

Dillard doesn't look old enough to have a thirteen-year-old son. His weak chin looks as though it never needs shaving.

"Do they attend school in Payne?"

"No, they live with their mother in Macon." Mr. Dillard clears his throat. His eyes shift toward the judge and then back to Ben. "We're getting divorced."

"I see. I am sorry to hear that." He is, I know. Because now Mr. Dillard isn't our upstanding respectable father of two, he is a man facing a life change, a future divorced dad. I put an *X* beside his name and write "divorce." A man with the breakup of his home on his mind is not the best candidate for a murder trial.

"Mr. Dillard, you realize that if convicted, the defendant could face the death penalty, and as a juror in our state, you would be responsible for prescribing that sentence. Now, I am not saying you will have to, but I have to ask, Mr. Dillard, would you be able to? Could you sentence a man to death?"

"If there were no other options?" I write another *X* next to Mr. Dillard's name and add "death penalty opposed." "If I had to, yes, I suppose I could."

Everyone will be asked this. If anyone says no, that person is excused. The ability to say yes, I can sentence someone to death, is called "death qualified." Funny to think I would not qualify. Funnier still, considering where I am sitting.

"Thank you, Mr. Dillard." Ben turns a fraction, so I may see his raised brows. I nod to indicate that I get it, that Mr. Dillard is out.

"Mrs. Clemens, how are you today?" Ben moves on to the next juror, a middle-aged black woman wearing a small gold cross. That cross could be good or bad, depending on her religious position. There are the merciful Christians who believe in the redemptive powers of establishing a relationship with their savior, Jesus Christ. These will not allow a lethal cocktail of pharmaceuticals to be injected into someone. Then there are the vengeful Christians who spout scriptures with messages of justice and vengeance. They will not hesitate to send another human to a final reckoning with God. The trouble lies in distinguishing between the two. When we spoke last week, over paper cups filled with coffee, Ben warned me that this distinguishing is not as easy as it appears. I wanted to say, "You think it's easy? Any of it?" I held it in.

Mrs. Clemens is fifty-two, married, and stays at home. She has an infant granddaughter named Eileen. Mrs. Clemens sings in the choir at her church, the First Baptist, on High Street. Not the First Baptist on New Street. I make a note of it. Maybe it will mean something to Ben. All it means to me is that Macon possesses more churches than gas stations, and that it needs to rethink its naming system. After all, you can only have one first anything.

Ben slides his eyes toward me. I stare back, my face set, body upright and a little stiff. I never should have quit ballet. It would have improved my courtroom posture. I jot a note down beside Mrs. Clemens's name. Actually it isn't a note. It's a doodle of a star. It doesn't mean anything. I am drawing so Ben will stop looking at me like a suspicious teacher checking on a recalcitrant pupil.

"Mrs. Clemens, do you believe a child who was abused may be more likely to commit crimes?"

"Yes, I suppose I do."

"And would you consider that history of abuse to explain criminal behavior? For example, would you favor leniency toward a defendant that had been abused as a child?"

"Well, now, I don't know." I watch Ben watch Mrs. Clemens. "There are plenty of abused children in this world. Too many, I fear, but not all of them grow up to be criminals. So it doesn't seem right to say that's why they done what they done, does it?"

I scribble a "yes" next to "mitigating circumstances: abuse." Yes means she is on our side. Mrs. Clemens looks good, or, by contrast, she doesn't look bad. "They should call it jury deselection," Ben whispered to me in the hallway before we entered the courtroom. "Since it's more about getting rid of the ones you don't like."

Ben's next questions concern whether she has any relationship to the defendant or victims. Mrs. Clemens admits she once attended a wedding at which Mr. Brown, Dominic's father, presided. Ben smiles; his entire face radiates goodwill for her honesty. When I give him honesty I never get a smile. My pen moves to make a mark beside Mrs. Clemens's name to indicate that we like her, but then I see I did so when I was doodling. She has a star beside her name. Huh. Maybe I should tell Ben I am able to divine our best jurors through doodling.

Ben thanks her and moves on to Mr. Gusswater, an out-of-work electrician from Macon. I tear my eyes from Mr. Gusswater's Adam's apple, which jumps up and down with every word spoken.

I look left, where defense attorney Mr. Thomas Landry, son of the almost Supreme Court contender, sits. His dark hair is slicked so it looks a bit like that of a Ken doll, plastic and stiff. That's where the resemblance to Ken ends. Thomas Landry is five shades darker than Ken and wears glasses that are only lacking a piece of the tape in the middle for geek authenticity. His bow tie, red, contrasts with the white dress shirt and navy blue suit.

"I can impose a death penalty," Mr. Gusswater says. He sounds like he is ready to pull the switch now. A star goes beside his name. An ideal juror for us, and a person I cannot respect.

I sneak another look at Landry. He is making notes of his own, though he has an aide beside him, some ruddy-cheeked lawyer who looks as though the ink on his degree is still wet. I didn't catch his name in the hallway when Landry stopped to introduce himself this morning.

"Miss Goldberg," he had half shouted. I turned at the unexpected summons. "How do you do? I am Thomas Landry." His voice was his best feature: a strong baritone that seemed too big for his body. He had civil engineer written all over him, and it wasn't just the eyeglasses.

"I have been a longtime admirer of your father's work," he said, setting his briefcase beside his leg. I noticed the laces on his black wingtips were loose. "Except for the Hallihan case. Didn't care for that one."

No shock there. Jeff Hallihan was a New England dairy farmer who argued for the segregation of Boy Scout troops. He figured since they could exclude gays, why not blacks? My father represented his case against the New Hampshire town where he lived, which had invoked a restraining order against Mr. Hallihan prohibiting him from getting closer than five hundred yards to any public school, town hall building, or public meeting space. He argued that the town's lockdown violated Mr. Hallihan's freedom of expression and his right to engage in free speech. He also showed that Mr. Hallihan's home had been searched without a warrant. He won the case.

"A lot of people didn't care for my father's representation of Hallihan. A lot of people didn't care for his representation of Gillison, either." If Landry was a fan, he would know that Gillison was the leader of a black protest group in the late 1970s who bombed a veterans' club outside Boston. My father defended him against charges of conspiracy and arson. He won the case, and proved, in the process, that several members of the police had tampered with and planted evidence. During the trial my mother and I stayed with friends in New York, on what I believed was a minivacation. My father wanted us safe from retaliatory measures. It wasn't until years later that I made the connection between the court decision and the date of our surprise summer trip.

I launched some retaliation of my own at Landry. "And I suppose a lot of people don't care for your representation of your client." I shrugged. "Nice meeting you."

"Thank you, Mr. Gusswater," Ben says in the voice parents use for their Little Leaguer sons. He is a go for us, although Landry will use a strike to remove him. There is no way he will keep a guy who sounds like the death penalty's number one fan.

Ben strolls before the jury box, asking questions, then stepping back to rest his hand against our table. He seems relaxed, at ease, as if he is chatting with friends in his living room. This persona, this appeal, is powerful. I almost fall victim to it myself. I place an X beside Lisa Kelsey's name. She mentions a brother in prison and appears reluctant to enforce the death penalty. She shifts in her seat as though it is too hot, though the temperature in the courtroom is, for once, mild.

Judge Pullman's gavel raps against wood twice after Miss Kelsey finishes. He announces a recess for lunch. My stomach awakens to these magic words, and a low gastric rumble rolls through me. Or maybe it is the anxiety of tallying people on a sheet that is gnawing at my stomach lining. Either way, I am happy for the opportunity to move my legs.

Ben and I eat across the street at the Between the Bread Cafe. He orders a roast beef sandwich, fries, and a milkshake. I have a chicken salad. He looks at my mixture of greens, veggies, and breast meat and says, "How can you survive on that?"

I stare at his plate full of food, dripping grease and ask, "How are you going to stay awake this afternoon?" Has he never experienced an afternoon food coma?

"What do you think so far?" he asks, after eating half his sandwich in three bites.

"Clemens and Gusswater seem good, but there is no way Landry will let Gusswater stay."

He wipes at the corner of his mouth with a paper napkin. "Not if he has any brains."

"Thought Landry was smart." My soda slurps through my straw. I look about to make sure no one has noticed. The other patrons are busy giving their orders to waitresses who wear pencils tucked behind their ears.

"Smart enough. What were you two talking about this morning?" He has finished his sandwich. His thick fingers scoop up multiple French fries and deposit them into his mouth.

"He introduced himself, said he was a fan of my father's work."

"He wasn't asking any questions about the case?"

"Why, Ben, are you protecting my legal virtue?" I infuse my question with as much saccharine as possible.

He grunts.

"I am capable of fending for myself," I tell him, checking the wall clock. We have fifteen minutes left.

"Just be careful," he warns. I repress a snort. Does he think Landry can fish information out of me? I could give him testimonials from several defense attorneys who will vouch that I keep my legal tricks hidden very far up my sleeves.

"Let's head back," he says, tossing money onto the tabletop. He waves aside my hand as I reach for my purse. "I will pay." He and I have always brought our own food to lunches so I am unsure whether this is collegial courtesy or Southern breeding.

"Thanks," I tell him before scooping up his last French fry. I pop it into my mouth and enjoy his crestfallen expression, as if that French fry was all that was standing between him and starvation.

"Told you I can fend for myself." I wind my way through the maze of metal chairs, toward the exit. Across the street, in the court, Justice waits for us to pick our teams.

Chapter Twenty-one

"So what's this, date number seven?"

"Eight," Lacey corrects.

"Lacey's got a boyfriend," I singsong. "Lacey and Todd, sitting in a tree, k-i-s-s-i-n-g."

"Stop it, you're embarrassing yourself," she scolds. "Good God, you sound like me."

I smile because she is right. "He's taking you to see *The Lion King*?"

"Yeah, he knows the director through the foundation somehow. I couldn't believe it when he said he got tickets."

My smile lingers as I wonder how Lacey, who has issues about suspension of disbelief in musicals, is going to handle a theatrical performance about singing and dancing animals. I decide against asking.

"So when are you coming to visit me and meet my beau?"

I am startled by the question and the anger behind it. "I don't know. I have this capital case. Maybe after that. I can't predict when it will end."

"You know I can work around your schedule. Just come. Say you'll come."

I almost ask why doesn't she come to me, but swallow the childish response. Todd is not in Macon and Lacey may feel awkward inviting him to Georgia to meet me, as if he must pass inspection.

"I'll come."

"Really?" Her squeal of excitement makes my ear hairs vibrate.

"Yes. Really."

Lacey talks of all the things we will do when I come: eat real bagels, visit the penguins at the Central Park Zoo, drink hot chocolate at Serendipity, and visit her new favorite clothing store in SoHo. As she catalogues our time together I see it before me: the metal spires of the Chrysler Building shining silver-gold in the sun. There will be yellow cabs crowding the streets, and the fragrant steamy smell of pretzels and hot dogs, with undertones of ketchup and pigeon urine. My house collapses about me to a third of its size and I stand within the eleventh-floor apartment I once rented for too much money. Henry James barks next door. Yes, yes, it's all there, behind my eyes and inside my stomach and under my callused heels.

I promise Lacey again that I will visit and leave her to plan an itinerary, knowing she will be distracted by another task within forty-five minutes. Not me, with my daily planner and self-adhesive notes stuck to the refrigerator reminding me to pick up dry cleaning. Lacey's system is fluid. She makes stuff up as she goes along. I have always liked that about her, though it baffles me. How can anyone live without knowing where she stored last year's tax returns?

I think forward, to seeing Lacey and returning to New York. Unlike Lacey, I never took to Manhattan. I didn't love it, not the way real New Yorkers do. I didn't worship at the temple of the Yankees or get fired up by local politics or care what constituted the next new "hot" thing. I rarely took advantage of the city's entertainments and I often felt suffocated by the swarms of people around me: on the trains, in restaurants, and at museums. The city shone too bright and blared too loud.

I never planned to live in New York forever. But to leave the way I did made me sad to go. The differences between it and Macon, so pronounced as to be tragicomic, only made me miss New York more than I might have had I ended up somewhere less unlike it.

I sigh and head to the kitchen where my dirty dishes await. One plate, a fork, a knife, and a glass. It does not seem worth opening the dishwasher door and arranging the items within the slots of plastic spikes. I turn on the tap and squeeze a yellow stream of dish soap into the metal sink, remembering how I used to complain about my lack of a dishwasher in New York.

Maybe I am never satisfied with what I have. Dishwasher/love/job/family. I hum under my breath, unaware of the song until I recognize the tune. "Satisfaction." I wipe the face of the plate with the dishrag, wide circles to little circles.

A sharp metallic chirp trills, and I nearly lose my grip on the plate. I steady it and settle it into the drying rack. The metallic chirp continues to berate me. I miss the phones of my youth, which rang in pure bell tones and sounded more like a wedding and less like a verbal harangue.

I rub the hot soapsuds off my hands with a dish towel. The phone's plastic feels cold. "Hello?"

"Natalie?" The low voice, once described as "sonorous" by a reporter writing for *The New Yorker,* startles me because it is the last voice I expect to hear.

"Dad?" It is absurd to ask, just as it was absurd for him to end my name with a question mark, as if we have forgotten what the other sounds like. As if we could. "Why are you calling? Is everything okay?" I picture my mother semireclined and unconscious on a hospital bed.

"Everything's fine. Nothing is the matter." It is the same thing he used to tell me when I protested that no, there really were monsters under my bed and inside my closet. "I just called to see how you were doing. We haven't talked in a while."

No kidding. "I'm fine. Good. Busy. You?"

"Things at the office are quiet now. Next month we have two big cases concerning student confidentiality."

"What kind of students?"

"Elementary school, high school, the ones too young to dispute having to submit to laws they cannot affect since they cannot vote." I know this speech well, having heard it many times. It once incited me to argue with the manager of a local CVS about the sales tax on a package of barrettes. Taxation without representation, I argued, was unfair. At thirteen I couldn't vote, but I was expected to pay taxes on everything from nail polish to restaurant pizza. The drugstore manager waived the tax, because he was tired of hearing me talk and I was holding up the line.

"Massachusetts?" I ask, referring to the venue where his cases will be heard.

"Vermont."

"Good luck."

"Thanks." He clears his throat. "I read about your upcoming case in the paper."

"Which one?" Stupid question. It must be the Washington trial.

"The capital case. It was in *The Boston Globe,* a footnote on the national news. You were listed as the prosecution."

Is he asking if it is true? Does he distrust the fact-checkers at the *Globe* or the Associated Press? "Jury selection began today." I rub the back of my neck, which feels like a rubber band stretched too far.

"How did it go?"

"Okay, I guess. Hard to tell. Juries are a crapshoot." Oy vey, I have just quoted Ben. "We hope to finish by tomorrow."

"Nervous?"

Oh. That question. My waist encircled by a pink tulle tutu, my hair pulled back, inside Miss Juliet's School of Dance. My pink-slippered feet reluctant to step forward onto the stage. "Nervous?" my dad asked, bending so that he could look into my eyes and see the fear himself. I loved the tutus, hair ribbons, and leotards but I did not love the recitals when everyone would watch me twirl and hop out of time with the other girls whose feet seemed surer, better placed than mine.

"Yes," I admit, just as I did then. "But I'm second-chairing. My colleague, Ben Maddox, will do most of the trial presentation."

"Do you know the defense?"

"Not really. His name is Thomas Landry. He says he admires your work, except for the Hallihan case. He didn't care for that one."

"You wouldn't think being a lawyer would have much in common with being a Broadway actor," he says. "But sometimes it feels that way, when people critique your performance as if it were a role. 'I loved you in *Walker* v. *Raymond* but hated you in *Mclellan* v. *Dresner*.' " His falsetto mocks someone but I don't know whom. The tightness of his voice surprises me. He never seemed bothered by the accusations of publicity-seeking or the description of him as a bloodhound on the scent of tomorrow's liberal cause. He used to laugh at the newspaper articles and unflattering mail.

"My cocounsel, Ben, knows the defense, or defense counsel's family, and in Georgia it's all about 'your people.' " I draw out the phrase in my best mock Southern accent, which isn't very good. My throat clips the long vowels short.

He does not respond to this. "I spoke to George Millner the other day. He was telling me that GLAAD is looking for another staff attorney. They are doing some interesting work on same-sex marriage cases in Massachusetts."

"That's great." I like George Millner. He lived across the street and consulted with my dad years ago. He often brought me stickers or candy when he stopped by. A man with two daughters, he knew how to bribe a little girl. "How is he doing? Didn't his younger daughter, Julia, get married recently?"

"He's doing well. Yes, Julia did get married, to an eye surgeon at Mass Eye and Ear. David something or other." I smile. My father cannot remember people's names unless he repeats them to himself like a mantra just after meeting them. "He asked about you and how you were doing."

"I hope you told him I'm well." The words eject themselves like bullets, harsher than I had intended. I rub my forehead with the heel of my hand.

"I told him about your work. He couldn't believe you were in Macon, or at the DA's office. I think he might have had you in mind when he told me about the GLAAD position."

I sit at the kitchen table and stop a sigh. It tickles. "I don't want to work for GLAAD."

"Why not? They do terrific work. Your mother would love to have you close again." I lean harder into the tabletop.

"Dad, do you remember when I took ballet?" I close my eyes and I am seven years old again and graceful as a three-legged buffalo.

"Yes. You were a beautiful sugarplum fairy." He is remembering the photo of me on the mantel. He may be looking at it now.

"But I hated ballet. I liked the outfits and some of the music. I did not like the classes or the teacher and I loathed recitals, remember?"

He chuckles. "You tried to convince your mother that you couldn't perform in the Winter Festival because you had chicken pox. You drew spots all over yourself with a blue Magic Marker."

"I couldn't find the red one," I protest, still anxious to make sure that it is understood that I intended to draw red spots, not blue ones. "But Dad, remember how I thought I would hate summer camp in Maine?"

"You cried every day for a week before you left. We almost didn't send you. Your poor mother sobbed her heart out on the drive home after we dropped you off."

"But I loved it. Remember?"

"How could I forget? You didn't want to leave. You had made so many friends and you even learned to fish." Me, the poster child for not getting dirty, had baited a hook and caught a fish. I made my camp counselor remove the fish from the line for me, though, certain the fish would try to exact vengeance.

"Well, life is like that. Sometimes the things you always wanted turn out to be less than you had hoped, and the things you dreaded become wonderful." I stare at the kitchen around me, at my collection of teacups, at my refrigerator sporting pastel sticky notes with to-do lists. "I am good at my job. I am helping people. Not the way I planned to, but I *am* still helping." Who am I trying to convince: him or me?

"But honey, you haven't even tried. You are so young. You only had the other job in New York, and I *know* that is not what you wanted. But now, you can do anything. You don't have to stay down there."

"I think I might."

"Natalie, you have been down there over a year now. You beat them at their game."

My scalp tingles. "What do you mean?"

"Nattie, you showed them what you are made of. You don't have to do it anymore. You won." I won? Won what?

He sighs, the same long exhalation he would make before telling me I had to eat my carrots or that I couldn't play outside after dinner. It is his patented "why must you make me say it" sigh. "Staying down there won't change anything. What is done is done. I think you have suffered enough. You can stop punishing yourself."

I stare before me at the small dish towel hanging from the handle of the oven. There is a tomato-sauce stain by the lower right corner.

He knows about Henry and the partners. I told him. It burst out of me during an argument over my plan to go to Macon. Judge Owens had spoken to him, given wind of my plan, before I had shared it. Dad called wanting to know why I had asked the judge to recommend me for a job in the South, and when I planned on telling him. He pointed out that my criminal law experience was limited at best.

"I need this job," I had told him.

A public prosecutor? In Georgia? Was I aware it was a death penalty state? Did I have any idea what the low salary would be? He threw questions at me like baseballs, hard, unrelenting.

"Dad, I slept with a partner at the firm. He accused me of screwing up an account, a major account. The partners wanted to demote me. I couldn't stay."

He was silent for so long I began to worry. When he spoke he said, "They cannot fire you. That is discrimination for a consensual act."

I wanted him to say, "Which partner? I will kill him." I wanted him to be my father, not a lawyer. His calm acceptance of my behavior disturbed me. I expected him to be shocked. I wanted him to be. Didn't he think better of me?

"Nattie? Are you there?" he says now.

I swallow and nod, although he cannot see me. "I'm here," I whisper.

"Nattie, think about George's offer. I know he would be glad to have you. He always wished one of his girls wanted to follow in his footsteps. He used to tell me how he envied me you."

I nod again. "Okay," I say because I cannot say more.

"Do you want to talk to your mother?" He offers her like a bandage, something to stop the bleeding. But I do not want her, not now.

"No. Tell her I love her. I will talk to her soon. I . . . I need to go to bed. It's a big day tomorrow."

"Okay, you take care now. Sweet dreams."

He ends the call with this invocation, as if he can summon visions of sugarplums and assign them to my bedside. I put the phone down and lean my chin onto hands splayed flat on the table.

I try to remember drawing those blue spots on my body with the marker. Did I only cover the areas exposed by my clothes or was I more thorough in my deceit? I do recall how flat and square the navy spots looked. I wasn't fooling anyone.

I shuffle to the bathroom, aware that it is the nights I need sleep most that I often find it hardest to obtain.

As I splash tepid water onto my face, I remember hearing my mother tell my father how I had tried to trick her with the marker. I had snuck down the hall to listen to them talking in the kitchen. My mother recounted how she found me with the uncapped marker and the family medical guide displaying chicken pox, how my body was covered in navy spots. She told him I had pled the Fifth Amendment when asked what I was doing. He had laughed, long and loud. When he recovered breath to speak he said, "That's my girl."

"She most certainly is," said my mother. "She is all yours."

Chapter Twenty-two

September 5, 2000

"We'll reconvene tomorrow at eight o'clock." Judge Pullman bangs his gavel twice and stands. His black robe flutters behind him as he escapes through the door set into the back wall. The bailiff announces that all should rise, and the jury members stir slowly, as if awakening from a decade-long slumber. Glazed eyes and stiff bodies turn toward the bailiff assigned to shepherd them from the room, to keep them safe from any press and outside influence. They follow in his wake like baby chicks behind their mother hen.

I reach for my satchel and grunt underneath my breath as I bend over. My feet hurt. They shouldn't, since I have been sitting all day. I must have been clenching my toes inside my too-tight pumps. Nerves. The first day of my first capital murder trial.

Ben stands, waiting for me, his right hand resting on the top of his briefcase. Landry sits at his table, staring ahead to where Judge Pullman sat a minute earlier. I wonder how he thought it went.

A few journalists have gathered on the courthouse steps looking to catch a five-second sound bite. Ben gives them a few hearty reassurances that we're going to win and remove the scourge that is Calvin Washington from the streets of Georgia so its citizens can sleep safely at night. My effort to blend into the steps meets with success. No reporters thrust their bulbous microphones into my face like feedbags to a horse. When Landry appears the microphones migrate and Ben and I make our way, unimpeded, to the street. We don't look back to watch Landry make his own vows to the public.

We head to the office. Ben's pace is slower than my own, but given his age, weight, medical condition, and Southern upbringing, this presents little surprise. Two blocks into our journey finds me wishing I had a pair of flip-flops hidden in my satchel.

Halfway to the office Ben says, "Landry's opening was solid."

I grunt, too tired to speak. Landry spoke of his client's innocence, harping on the lack of the murder weapon and the police department's failure to pursue other suspects. He added comments about his client's poor upbringing: his learning disability (dyslexia), his broken home (father left when Calvin was four), and his abuse at the hands of his violent stepfather and subsequent foster parents. A few jurors shot curious looks at Calvin's dark, impassive face. I spotted more than one juror's face wrinkling with thought as Landry hinted that this prosecution was just another in a series of fate's cruel tricks against Calvin Washington.

The dark brick of our building appears. I ignore the screaming lines of pain radiating from my toes to my heels. "You were better," I say.

Ben slows his gait, which is somewhat tilted to one side and rolling, as if he is standing on a ship. He tilts his head toward me. "What's that?" I can't tell if he genuinely misheard me, lost in courtroom abstractions, or if he is merely making me repeat myself.

"I said your opening was better." Just half a block now and we will be inside. I have a pair of soft, slip-on mules in my closet.

"Why do you say that?"

I grimace. Clearly he wants all I will give. "You laid it all out easy-peasy. You didn't lose one of them. They hung on your every word, and they stared at Washington as if checking him for horns. You had them questioning everything Landry had told them."

Ben smiles. "He sure did have them leaning forward when he described the gun's absence, though," he points out.

"It's a murder trial, not a game of lost and found. Just because we didn't find the gun doesn't mean we lose." I hope the jury realizes this.

I hobble toward the building, salvation within sight. Ben holds the door for me, and I stumble past George who greets us with a "good evening." We wait before the elevator bank, and, though I hate the moving box of imminent death, I do not for a minute consider taking the stairs.

"Wilkins did well on the stand," Ben muses. The elevator announces its approach with a squeal of metal and the smell of burning rubber. "Better than Cox might have done."

The metal jaws open. Ben follows me inside. The doors close with cinematic slowness. I keep my gaze trained on the buttons and try to concentrate on the image of the navy blue slip-ons waiting for me on my closet floor. Ben hums under his breath. I almost stumble and trip when the doors creak open, for I realize he is humming a Frank Sinatra song, "Chicago." It is one of Lala's flower song standards.

I hurry to my office and the promise of podiatric relief. Ben's hand on my arm halts my forward progress. "What?" I ask, in a tone that demands a good explanation.

He favors me with a cool glance. The sort he shot toward Landry all day long. "The case is moving forward quickly, despite all of Landry's objections. We may rest as early as Thursday. You ready to cross Mr. Gentry?" His soft brown eyes examine me. I straighten my shoulders and stand taller.

"I hope so." Damn. That is not what I meant to say. I meant to say yes, absolutely, no doubt, I am ready.

"I hope so, too." He moves his briefcase from his left hand to his right. "See you tomorrow morning. Seven-thirty."

I nod. Then I hurry past everyone in the hall, keeping my head low so I won't have to stop and talk. The few people still about do not interrupt me, aware that I've been in court all day trying a capital case. It's a bit like being a pitcher with a no-hitter game going, or so Carl has explained. Some weird baseball voodoo superstition thing. I offer silent thanks to its law equivalent.

I drop my satchel beside my desk and walk to the closet, flinging the door against the wall in my enthusiasm. I bend down, look inside, and blink hard. Leaning forward and twisting my torso, I peer into dusty corners where no shoes could possibly hide. I stand and rise to search the shelf where boxes of office supplies are organized by function, shape, and color.

My right palm smacks my forehead when memory returns. I wore the shoes home last week, after a late-night prep session with Ben. I am enraged for a moment with the me of a week ago. My feet did not hurt that night, not like now. Now I could weep from the throbbing in my toes. I step out of the shoes and slowly flex them, wincing as the movement increases and releases the tension. Ow, ow, ow.

I look about the room and decide my e-mail and phone messages can wait. I step back into the prison of my shoes and cross the room for my briefcase. The dark green and wood of the room are too much now. I crave the soft colors of my home.

A rectangle of light illuminates the carpet before Ben's open office door. He is still inside, working. He should go home. No unexpected developments require he remain, and he could use the rest. The pouches under his eyes have sagged to new depths. I consider sticking my head into his office and telling him to go, but that might only make him stay later. He is as bad as I am that way.

He was good in court today, really good, assertive and convincing, but engaging and seemingly kind. He didn't deny Landry's statements that his client had suffered at the hands of the foster home system or juvenile courts. He did not do what many prosecutors would have done: demand that the handcuffed man in the courtroom be considered a monster. He did something much smarter. He admitted Calvin Washington was human, and he played on this notion of humanity, of frailty, passion, violence, and its consequences until he had the jury believing that humans are hazardous creatures and the removal of the most dangerous was necessary to the preservation of society. An old-new notion expounded by philosophers from Plato to Kant. But Ben managed to incorporate this idea and encapsulate it so that it could be swallowed, without water, by a box of twelve critics. Hardest of all, he managed to do this on his feet. I heard bits of his prepared opening, and, with the exception of the names of the victims and the defendant, it was wholly different. The first version contained lots of "cold-blooded" and "inhuman" references. Within the time it took for him to listen to Landry's pathos-heavy opening, he revised his entire speech. He toned down the anger and belligerence and made it more effective for its lack of huff and puff.

As I slide into my car seat and close the door with a soft thud I realize that I have spent the past five minutes engaged in admiring the courtroom skills of one Mr. Benjamin Maddox. So enraptured by the memory of his devastating put-down of Landry as his "soft-hearted colleague, corrupted by the idea of corruption, enslaved by the notion of conspiracy theories," I managed to forget my elevator fear.

Cool night air sweeps through the window and ruffles the collar of my shirt. Soon it will be my turn to stand in the courtroom, to cross-examine Abraham Gentry, the witness who claims to have seen Calvin Washington at a gas station in Columbus near the estimated time of the murders. It seems unlikely Calvin Washington could have killed two people and have been spotted in Columbus forty-five minutes later. It will be my job to make sure the jury is left with no doubts, reasonable or otherwise, as to the veracity of Mr. Gentry's story. My stomach clenches. I can't screw up. I won't.

On my street, the houses glow, lit from within, like jack-o'-lanterns. The Gessler twins' toppled bicycles lie on their front lawn, fallen to their sides. I imagine the children hopping off their bikes and letting them fall where they may as they race each other inside. I think of Sarah's children, Billy and Lily. Are they riding bikes at their great-aunt's house? Have they stopped asking when Daddy will come?

No lights shine from my white box house. The yellow shutters look like dark wings attached to the bodies of the windows in the evening dark. The gutter is hanging too low on the right side. I ought to have it repaired.

I kick the shoes off my feet as soon as I am inside. The right one misses the hall lamp by centimeters. I pick up my slippers at the side of the bed, where I stepped out of them and into my horrible shoes this morning. The slippers laugh at me, pink and fluffy, with tiny bunny ears poking up and out. A purchase inspired by whimsy. They seemed so silly, so impractical, so very unlike me.

I slip-slap my way into the kitchen and peer into my freezer. I need a prepackaged meal option that will require five minutes or less in the microwave. Frozen chicken curry. Perfect. Now for a drink. Wine. Red? I bend to root through my wine cage. It holds a maximum of sixteen bottles. Now it contains only three. My nose wrinkles. Weren't there five bottles the other day? And where did the Australian Shiraz go? I grab the lowermost bottle, a Riesling, and settle it atop the table, banishing thoughts of alcoholism for now.

I consume a too-soft chicken piece that dissolves like aspirin in my mouth. I chase it with the Riesling, which is not the best I've ever had, or even a close fourth. Where did the damn Shiraz go?

I finish my second glass of wine, dutiful in taking my medicine. It helps me sleep, and lately I need my sleep. Sometimes when I close my eyes and press my fingertips against my lids I see starbursts, flashes of white against a dark background. One day in November, I sat at my desk, head in my hands. I touched my fingertips to my closed lids and I didn't see starbursts. I saw a mutilated woman. Her face swollen with bruises, her temple dark with blood. Her hair twisted behind her as if trying to escape. The worst of it was that she was alive, unconscious, but alive.

The photo sat atop Carl's desk, in a folder. He saw me look at it as I approached to ask him a question. He closed the folder and apologized. Carl is careful not to expose outsiders to the brutality of his work. Back then, still awaiting the results of my Georgia bar exam, I was very much an outsider. But the flash of that woman inside my skull brought me one step closer to the legions of attorneys who sleep too little and drink too much, who talk about sports or cars or politics because talking about justice is impossible.

The woman behind my eyelids appeared once. Yet how easily might a fellow victim of violence appear when my eyes are closed? Each day the number of casualties increases. I don't know what scares me more: that I will see them behind my lids, or that I will grow so used to them that, even behind my pupils, they cannot shock me?

I close the dishwasher and head for the bathroom. I try not to stare at the blue shadows underneath my eyes, or the zit near my hairline. The toothpaste tube requires a lot of squeezing. I brush, up down, up down, until the egg timer tells me I can stop. My soap pump coughs forth a handful of foam only after I hit it several times with my right palm. Its plastic body gasps and wheezes. When was the last time I visited the drugstore? My head struggles to remember and gives up. It feels fuzzy and padded with cotton wool, a good omen for sleep.

In my bed I draw the covers up to my chin, refusing to submerge myself further because it makes me claustrophobic. The moon is a crescent in the blue-purple sky. I try to fix the image in my head so that when I sleep I will see its benign glow. I hope it might banish any darker images within my mind.

Chapter Twenty-three

September 8, 2000

"Life is meant for living," I say, an expression favored by my mom. She reserved it for my busy father when he would contend he could not eat, see a movie, sleep, or visit friends.

This week Ben and I have been inside the courthouse each day, all day, or most of it, and it is wearing me down. Watching the jurors' faces for signs of points won or lost, listening to the judge overrule Landry's objections, searching Ben's face and body for signs of illness. Dominic's parents, Emily and Douglas, sit behind me every day, eyes forward, hands clenched, shoulders slumped. The oversized photographs, increased in size to show all the horrific details of Marcus's beating, make me lose my appetite for lunch and dinner.

I want to forget it all. That is why I am applying lipstick, making that ridiculous fish face women do. It is why I am leaving to go to Jessup's, a bar music club.

My bag sails behind me as I exit the bathroom, and I am moving so fast that I do not see Ben until I collide with him. My chest hits his arm and I step back, electrified, seized with horror that his left arm now knows what my right breast feels like.

"Whoa," he says, hands up, palms out.

"Sorry," I mumble.

"What's your hurry? Big date?" He squints at my change of clothes.

"No."

"Well, have a nice time wherever you're going." He steps forward, toward his office, his slow shuffle implying that some people never rest in their pursuit of justice.

"I'll be sure to give Helen your regards," I call out as I saunter away.

"Helen?" He has stopped and is frowning at me.

"Helen Leland. You know, the reason God made miniskirts?"

His face melts like an overheated ice-cream cone. I turn my back on its comic promise and leave before he can say anything in his defense.

Helen invited me, via a message left on my home phone, to hear her friend's band. She found my unlisted telephone number, resourceful girl. I called with a politely worded refusal crammed full of trial-related excuses. I soon discovered that social coordinator Helen Leland made defense attorney Helen Leland look like a Girl Scout. She demolished my protests about having too much work, made several pointed comments about my lack of social life, and promised me entertainment the likes of which I had never experienced.

As I pull my car into the deeply pitted blacktop of the club's parking lot I begin to reevaluate Helen's promise. Could this be right? The name on the faded wooden building reads JESSUP'S. My fists seize with reluctance on the steering wheel. "Life is meant for living," I mutter. I turn the keys, grab my purse, and exit the car, double-checking the locks.

My half-jog stutters to a stop when I reach the door. Inside, I hear Patsy Cline wailing about being crazy. Across the threshold is a smoky room lit by out-of-season Christmas lights hung above a long bar. People crowd its wooden surface. Features are difficult to distinguish.

"Natalie!" Above the bar a hand is raised high, and I follow it to Helen, who sits atop a stool. She wears jeans and a top cut low enough to require a demibra. Her hair is pulled back into a ponytail and her eyes are rimmed in kohl like an ancient Egyptian's. I might have walked past her without knowing her.

She nods to a stool upon which her black boots rest. "Sit," she orders, in a cheerful voice, swinging her legs down.

I obey. A wave brings the bartender to us. Built on mastodon proportions, he slings a white dish towel over his shoulder. The snake tattoo on his forearm writhes. He rests his splayed fingers on the bartop, leans forward, and asks, "What can I get you?" His peppermint-scented breath surprises me.

My hesitation allows Helen to continue playing chief. "Two mint juleps," she says.

The bartender steps back to do her bidding and I glance about, repressing a cough. Most of the people look local. There are no brightly patterned shirts that mark tourists as effectively as name tags. I have yet to figure out why visitors feel they have to dress like elderly Floridians.

"Natalie, this is Pete," Helen says, introducing me to the impish man to her right. He looks like a leprechaun, from his red hair to his green tie. His freckles form small continents on his face.

"Hi, Natalie," he says, his voice absent of Ireland. Pure Georgia, low and drawly.

"And this is Flora and Hank," Helen continues, gesturing to the couple beside Pete. "And Frank and Ellen and Gary and Lorraine and Elisabeth."

I smile wide and nod after each name is spoken.

When my drink arrives I reach for my purse. Helen smacks my hand. "You can get the next one," she says.

She raises her glass, says, "To victory," and clinks her glass against mine. I assume she means in the courtroom.

I take a sip and Helen smiles. "Best mint juleps outside of my Cousin Buttercup's." My raised brows say "Buttercup?" Her ponytail wags affirmation. "That's nothing. Her sister is known as 'Honeydew' and the best thing is that their real names are Eugenia and Bessamine."

Lorraine, overhearing, shares a story about her best friend named Katherine, who was known as Kit to everyone and who fell in love with a man by the name of Katt. "The worst thing is that now people just call her 'Candy' or 'Chocolate,' " she said. Is Kit Katt black like Lorraine? I wonder.

Helen sees my frown and smiles. "Yes, Nat, she's African American." She draws out the designation to make it sound silly. She turns to Lorraine to confide, "Nat is a Yankee and therefore sensitive to such matters."

Lorraine bares her teeth. "Uh-huh," she says. "I lived in Delaware for a few months. Hated it."

I debate defending accusations of hailing from Delaware but decide it does not matter. Besides, Helen has a point. I have a difficult time discussing race. A product of New England liberalism, I was taught it was a matter discussed in the classroom, not outside.

"So do you like zydeco music?" Pete asks me, prompting a shrug. I have no idea. He begins to explain its origins. My focus is diluted by the increasing heat and noise.

A loud, sharp twang precedes a call of "Test, *un, deux, trois*" from the stage. Several people begin clapping and cheering. Half of Helen's entourage walks to the stage where a drummer, bassist, and roadie stand. Pete goes with them. I realize Helen doesn't just know a band member or two. She is with the band.

"You like to dance?" she shouts into my ear, her breath warm and sweet.

"Yes, but I have no rhythm."

Her smile is sirenous, capable of luring dead men to dance. "Great."

"Do you come here often?" I ask her.

"Not often enough. I used to live here in my teens." She looks about the bar as if checking it for changes. "This is where I met a few of those guys." Her ponytail bobs up as she leans forward. "They've been playing forever."

My own teenage years were spent in car pools, being shuffled from debate team matches and yearbook meetings or to the nearest T stop where my friends and I would travel to the movie featuring the latest teen heartthrob.

"So, Nat, what brought you to Macon?" Her words catch up to me a few seconds after she speaks them, the result of audio interference from the tuning band.

My heart stops, as it always does when confronted with this question. I am about to deliver my standard "the city became too much for me, I hated corporate law" spiel but she rips the stool from underneath me with her, "What sent you running away? Did you fuck up a huge account? Or was it something worse, like love?"

Unable to speak, I stare at her blue eyes, surrounded by black liner. How did she know?

"I'd put my money on love," she says as she turns to find the bartender. He finishes making change for two customers at the other end of the bar before lumbering over to us. I bet he has never hurried anywhere. He may, in fact, be incapable of hurrying.

"Yeah," I say, my voice croaky with secondhand smoke.

"Men are pigs," she says. She swivels her stool to say to our bartender, "Not you, Mikey. You're too big to be a pig. A badly behaved wild boar perhaps." Mikey's mouth extends a millimeter in either direction, his version of a smile.

I swallow a large sip of my second drink after laying a twenty on the bar for him to transform into a handful of singles.

"So you left New York brokenhearted, huh?"

Her smile seems cruel until she explains, "Everyone wondered when you showed up, what the hell you were doing here. Aaron Goldberg's daughter. Some of the people in the DA's office thought you were infiltrating the system to take it down, some sort of 'civil rights meets conspiracy theory' thing. You kept up that lame excuse of wanting a change from New York." Her grin tells me what she thought of that idea. The frosty looks, the reticent hellos during my first few weeks, all along I had assumed they were the result of being a Northerner, an outsider, a woman, a Jew. And it turns out they were afraid, unsure why I had come.

"Not me. I figured anyone tired of New York wouldn't choose Macon."

She is right, of course, and why this has not struck me as obvious I do not know. I wanted so badly for others to believe my cotton-candy lies that I failed to check if the story I constructed was too sweet and insubstantial to consume.

"You didn't seem inclined to a career in the DA's office." She grins. "But nowadays you come striding out of that courthouse looking like God himself appointed you to the prosecution." She leans back and hums under her breath. I cannot catch the tune because the accordion and harmonica have joined to create a duet.

Her insight renders me speechless. Does her X chromosome account for this wisdom or is experience lending her a hand? The "men are pigs" comment makes me wonder. "Let's dance," she says, "before the floor gets too crowded."

Is she kidding? There are only three people on the floor, shuffling to the accordion-heavy music. "It's going to fill fast. Trust me." She grabs my wrist and tugs me from my perch. Oddly, I do trust her. She sits at the opposite table during trials and she does not seem the nurturing sort, but I find myself trusting her all the same. She knew all along why I came to Macon and she didn't say anything.

The band is like none I have ever seen or heard. There is an accordion player, a drummer, two guitarists, two singers (one armed with a cowbell), a keyboardist, and a man wearing a ribbed piece of metal. He has two sticks that he rubs up and down the metal, creating a funny zippity-zap sound. Helen's friend Elisabeth notes my fascination with the musical armor. "It's a vest frottoir," she explains, causing me to search the recesses of my French-language memory. "A rub board," she adds. "It's what makes zydeco music zydeco." She smiles. "Here, move your hips more, bend your knees down like this." She demonstrates a move that seems impossible or, at the least, very dangerous. "Zydeco has its own dance style." She nods to my right. "Helen is a champ. Watch her and you'll pick it up."

Helen bends down with incredible speed and fervor. Her hips rotate like a dreidel spinning out of control. Her ponytail bounces and swings. Every male in the club and most of the women watch as she moves, and she ignores them all, eyes closed.

"Oh, sure. Just watch her. No problem."

Elisabeth laughs at my tone. She demonstrates how to step forward, turn, and bend. I try it and knock into the man beside me. "I'm hopeless," I confess.

"No. Dancing is about happiness. You don't have to follow steps. See?" She points to a couple who appear to be dancing a jitterbug.

I decide I would rather have one more drink. When I reach the bar Mikey stands, arms like slabs of meat, crossed against his chest. He watches the dancers, but I cannot tell if he is amused, interested, or bored. "May I have another mint julep?"

"You don't like to dance?" he asks, grabbing a glass from under the bar.

"Dancing doesn't like me," I tell him. "Never has."

That same fractional smile appears on his face as he places the drink before me. He waves away my money. "This one is on the house," he tells me in a tone that robs me of any response except "thank you."

Helen was right. The dance floor fills fast. Couples and individuals bop along to the crazy rhythms. Pete, the leprechaun, plays drums in the band and he winks at me halfway through a song, causing me to raise my glass in salute. The Christmas lights twinkle in my ice cubes. I close my eyes and breathe in the scent of gin, sweat, smoke, and grapefruit. Grapefruit? I open my eyes to see Helen standing before me, panting. She is the source of the citrus scent. Before I can ask what perfume she is wearing she hauls me to my feet.

"C'mon, lush," she says, tugging harder when I dig my heels into the sticky floor.

"Uh-uh," I tell her. "I can't do what you're doing out there. Besides, it's more fun to watch."

Accepting my mulish resistance for what it is, she hops atop her abandoned bar stool and tells Mikey to tell her friend to dance. Mikey's snake ripples as he wipes a tumbler clean.

"Nope," he says, setting the glass down and picking up another from the damp wood behind him.

Her brows rise an inch. "What did you do to win his heart?" she demands, swiveling her stool top in time to the music, unable to stop dancing even while seated.

"Nothing."

"He usually does what I tell him. Men." A lot of weariness is contained in that final syllable. "So what was wrong with Mr. New York, anyway?" She picks up our predance conversation like a mislaid beat.

The tumbler is cold beneath my fingers. I push it from me.

"He was married and a liar," I say, staring into the small mirror behind the bar. It allows me a glimpse of the back of Mikey's right shoulder moving forward in small circles as he rubs at a glass. Just beside his shoulder is a portion of my face: lit yellow and red by the lights above. My lipstick has not survived.

"Ugh," she mutters. "Did he promise he would leave his wife and marry you?"

I shake my head, glad that Mikey has moved down the bar to attend to some thirsty dancers.

"Well, that's something, then. Nothing like an unfaithful man making marriage promises to turn your stomach." Against my will I smile. Her matter-of-fact pronouncement, delivered in her honeyed voice, seems funny. I laugh.

"You know that ruby ring auctioned at Hay House?"

She stops swiveling and scrunches her face. "Yeah," she says.

"That was a gift from him."

Now it is her turn to laugh. "Good for you. And for a good cause, too. Even better." She leaves her stool. "One dance," she says. "Just one." She holds up her forefinger. "I'll show you."

"I am hopeless," I tell her but she is already ahead of me, stepping fast, clearing a path before her. I follow in her wake and tell myself that just one dance will be okay. I can do it, maybe.

Chapter Twenty-four

September 10, 2000

The wind is picking up. The heads of the swamp sunflowers bob, and their small yellow petals quiver in the breeze. I tell Lala that I always thought sunflower seeds resembled eyes. She sits across from me, sipping a cup of coffee and brandy. I hold a matching mug in my hand. We are enjoying the dregs of Sunday evening. I should be indoors, but I could not resist the flowers.

"Found a cantaloupe in the tomatoes this morning," she says, squinting at the vegetable garden. "Complete surprise. I didn't plant cantaloupes."

"You grew a cantaloupe by accident?"

"Yup."

"A real cantaloupe? By accident? Well, ain't that berries!"

Lala smiles at my use of one of her favorite phrases. "They are called volunteers." She sips her coffee and smiles.

"What?"

"Seedlings that take root where you don't intend them to grow. Misplaced seeds a bird drops or the wind scatters, or a fruit or vegetable in your compost pile that reproduces. They are called volunteers, accidental transplants."

"Accidental transplants," I repeat.

"The cantaloupe sprouted from one I had thrown onto my compost. If I had weeded the tomato section better it would have died, but as it is, it grew and I had a treat for breakfast."

"You ate it?" I cannot keep the disappointment from my voice.

"There is a piece left if you would like some." She begins to rise.

"No, no, I'm not hungry. Sit. Please. I just wondered what it looked like."

"Like any other cantaloupe, perhaps a little smaller. Tasted mighty fine."

"Not as good as your coffee, I'm sure." I wonder if Helen drinks coffee this way, if it's a Southern thing, or merely a Lala thing.

"Better than those fancy coffee drinks people pay four dollars for." She sips her drink to prove her point.

The hum of nearby bees makes me drowsy, that and the brandy. I wonder whether bees like alcohol or only alcohol that tastes sweet or maybe it doesn't matter. Lala rouses me from my mazy mental wanderings. "Nat, there's someone at your door."

I turn to look over the gate at my front door but the blooming Aussie Plume's thick, ribbed leaves obscure my view. "Probably Jehovah's Witnesses or Girl Scouts," I tell Lala. "I'll just be a minute."

When I reach my front yard I see that there is only one person at my door. Proselytizers tend to travel in pairs, and Girl Scouts are far younger than the woman standing on my steps. She turns as I say "Can I help you?" and I see her face. Sarah, Carl's sister. She carries a giant straw bag on her shoulder, big enough to carry an infant.

"Miss Goldberg?" She shadows her eyes with her hand. I am standing in the setting sun.

"Sarah, is everything okay?" In front of the house is a small blue compact car, not the minivan Sarah drove to the shelter.

"Everything is fine." She sees where I am looking and gestures toward the car. "That's my aunt's." After a brief hesitation she asks, "Could I speak with you?"

"Sure," I say, wiping my palms against the front of my shorts. I feel exposed, in my play clothes, in my yard, an ordinary woman on a Sunday.

I tell her to follow me and backtrack to Lala's. I told Lala I would return. Besides, the notion of inviting Sarah into my home disturbs me. I am reluctant to reveal my life to her, conscious of my hypocrisy. I barged into her home and life without so much as a by-your-leave.

She follows me through the gate, claps her hands together and exclaims, "Oh! How lovely!" I am pleased by her admiration. Lala's garden deserves it.

"Lala, I brought . . . a friend." How else to introduce Sarah?

Lala looks at me before rising to say "How do you do?" I wag my head a little and she says, "Would you like a drink? I won't be a minute." Before Sarah can respond, Lala is headed for the house. Wonderful Lala, catching my signal. I think Sarah and I might need a little privacy.

Sarah has to peer into the fishpond and look at the rocks surrounding the pool before she sits. I explain about the rocks, how Lala's friends gather them and bring them to her.

She asks a few questions about the neighborhood and how long I have lived in it. I surprise myself with my response. "Fourteen months." Has it really been so long?

"How nice," she says.

I wonder when she will talk about whatever it is that made her drive all this way to see me. Her face is whole again, unmarred by bruises. She is pretty, but her eyes are worried. I wonder if that will ever change.

I ask about the children. She tells me that they are well, and making friends in their new school. She was worried about registering them, unsure how to explain her status as not-quite-single parent to the schoolteachers and principal. "I found out I'm not the only mom in the school system with the same problem. There is another woman, Mabel Damon." She pauses and looks at me, as if expecting I know her.

"Has William done anything?"

"Except try to prove I'm crazy so he can take the children away?" Her laugh is brittle. "No, nothing. I'm drawing up divorce papers. I expect he may try something when he gets them. Although . . ."

"What?"

"Well, he did kill Captain, the dog." She brushes a spot beneath her eyes.

"I'm sorry. I'm so very sorry." I am, for Sarah and the kids and most especially Captain, who was only a dog and had no idea what he had done to drive his master into a rage.

"I didn't come to tell you that. I came because I wanted to explain. I . . . didn't . . . I wasn't . . ." She exhales, a long whoosh of air.

"Take your time," I tell her.

She leans forward, and I notice her feet are tiny, smaller than mine.

"I wasn't very nice to you, when you came. I was upset and angry and scared, especially for the kids. William had been worse lately. The week before you came he grabbed Billy by the back of his shirt and pushed him toward the counter, hard. Billy managed to stop himself from hitting the counter, but it was close." She shudders. "He had never hurt the kids before."

Just you, I think.

"When you came, well, it seemed like a sign. I knew everything you said was true. I was just afraid to leave him."

"I understand."

"Anyway, I never said thank you. Carl said he and Mom got you a present."

"Yes." I lift the chai from my neck so she can see it. "It's the Jewish symbol for life."

Sarah nods. "Our maternal grandmother was Jewish."

I am surprised. Carl is part Jew?

"Our grandfather didn't convert, and neither did she. I remember visiting them for holidays when I was very little. There was a Christmas tree and a menorah." She smiles. "William freaked out when he heard about Grandma Sarah. Said he didn't know he had married a Jew." Her smile disappears, and she turns an apologetic face to me.

"I've heard worse." I have, from people whose opinions matter more than William's.

"I came here to say thank you, and to give you something." She fishes in her bag and withdraws a tissue-wrapped rectangle that is creased and taped in many different places. "The kids wrapped it."

They sure did. It takes me half a minute to tear apart the tissue to reveal a photograph of Billy, Lily, and Sarah, standing in front of a petting zoo. The kids stand on either side of their mother, faces sticky with some treat, grinning. They look happy.

"Our new family photograph," she says.

"Thank you."

Lala calls out from the back porch. "Thirsty?" She holds a wicker tray loaded with several glasses. I hurry forward to take it from her. Lala says, "I brought a selection. Lemonade, iced tea, or coffee and juice."

"Coffee and juice?" Sarah's nose wrinkles.

"Brandy," I explain. "It's what we're drinking."

"Oh, I'll have iced tea, since I have to drive back."

"Would you like to stay to dinner?" Lala asks. I marvel at her easy acceptance of visitors. It is a Southern trait I wish I came by.

"I have to get back soon. I'm helping sew costumes for the kids' school play."

"I remember sewing school costumes," Lala says. "I made the mistake of being rather skilled with needle and thread. Years after my children left school I would receive calls from their former teachers asking if I might spare some time for the school pageant." She sips her mug. "It was fun seeing the children in those outfits."

I have no sewing stories to share. No kids-in-costume tales, either.

Lala and Sarah reminisce about favorite costumes and I rub the faux gold picture frame between my thumb and forefinger. Evening falls around us. Bugs sing and the sunflowers begin disappearing in the dusk.

"I should really go," Sarah says.

"It's been lovely talking with you. Come again, and bring your children," Lala says.

I tell Lala I will be back to wash out my mug. She says "Pshaw," and promises to let me wash up another day.

Sarah follows me to my yard. We stand outside her car. "Would you like to come inside?" I ask. "Use the bathroom?" She has another two hours of driving ahead of her.

"No, thank you." She jiggles her keys in her palm and tilts her head toward the house. "This is a lovely house. Do you own it?"

"No, I rent, although my landlady wants to sell and she has offered me first dibs."

"You should take it. The garden next door is worth it."

"I haven't decided yet."

She does not say anything more and I feel awkward for resisting her suggestion. Instead I thank her for visiting and say, "I . . . well, I felt bad about how I treated you that day. I wasn't very nice. I just pushed and pushed."

"I needed the push." She steps forward and gives me a hug. Her thin arms have muscles mine do not. She smells like vanilla and powder.

"If you want to stop by sometime," I begin. How is it Lala issues invitations so easily, so graciously? Why can't I?

"Maybe we will. The kids would love to see their uncle Carl. He spoils them."

"And Sarah, I am very sorry about Captain. I wish—"

"I know," she says.

I watch her get in her car and drive away until her taillights disappear around the corner. Then I enter the house that I cannot commit to buying because I am imprisoned in limbo.

When I came to Macon it was the result of a decision made in the heat of anger, inspired by Henry's duplicity and Walter's and MacLittle's smugness. I would show them. I would become a public prosecutor. Stupid to think I could make an impact on those men. Do they even remember my name?

I turned my life upside down, and now . . . now what? I have alienated my parents and disappointed my father. I am embroiled in a capital murder trial, prosecuting alongside a conservative Southerner who reduces me to muttering Yiddish phrases. In my spare time I become involved in a domestic abuse case that follows me home. I am learning about zydeco music and gardening and how to drink coffee and juice. I have destroyed all hope of completing the life plan I drew up at age fifteen.

I cannot be the famous civil liberties lawyer my father is, and I no longer want to be. My work is as important. I can safeguard the living from threats of violence; I can work to avenge the dead. I can protect the wounded from future harm, or try.

Can I live here, in Macon, Georgia, permanently? In a place where my whiteness makes me a minority? Where the death penalty laws I uphold set my teeth on edge?

Maybe I am a volunteer, like Lala's accidental cantaloupe. My path was supposed to lead elsewhere, but here I am.

I fetch a glass of water and settle into my favorite armchair. Beside it is the Gentry deposition. I found a flaw in it. Tomorrow Ben and I will discuss it before we head for the courthouse. I squint at the small print and try to concentrate, forgetting everything else: Sarah, my landlady, Ben, and especially Captain, the dog I couldn't save.

Chapter Twenty-five

September 13, 2000

Judge Pullman assigns a high value to food. Rather than transition from the prosecution resting to the defense's start, he decides to break for lunch. Ben and I discuss whether it is better that the jurors spend the next ninety minutes contemplating our work, or if it would have been preferable to begin dismantling the defense's case immediately. We talk on the way to the office, where we agree to spend our extended lunch catching up on other cases.

Before I can reach the sanctum of my office I encounter Carl. He sees me and waves. Then he begins tapping a folder against his chest. Is he ever still? "Hi," I say, walking fast.

"Hi, Nat. How are you?"

"Good." I keep walking.

"Um, Nat?" He is following me. Damn.

"Yes?" I turn around. His Bermuda-acquired tan looks fantastic against his light gray suit, and his hair is streaked even blonder. My brain cannot help but remind me, at this moment, that Carl is part Jew.

"Sarah called last night. She said she visited you?"

"Yes."

"She seemed okay? She sounded good, on the phone, but—"

"She seemed to be doing very well. It was good to see her."

"I'm glad." He is still tapping the folder against his chest.

"I've gotta go. I'm on lunch break and I have tons to catch up on." I glance at my watch.

"Right, sorry. I just wanted to check. Thanks again."

"It's going to be okay, Carl." I step forward and squeeze his arm. His bicep tenses beneath my hand.

He nods and steps back. I notice he has stopped tapping that damn folder, at last.

At my desk, my attention wanders from a police investigation into a recent armed burglary to my computer's monitor, which whirls through the artificial cosmos of a screen-saver pattern. I touch the mouse, and the stars disappear. Online I search airline prices. Atlanta to New York. Three hundred dollars seems to be the average, unless I am willing to connect through Chicago. I am not.

My finger hovers over the mouse. The arrow hangs over the button that will bring me to a new flight search. I tap the mouse, so gently nothing happens. I tap it harder, angered by my own indecision. New York to Boston. An hour-and-six-minute flight from La Guardia to Logan. I haven't been home since Hanukkah last year, and I kept that visit to two days because I was assisting on a manslaughter case. The stilted conversation about my new job, my new place, my new friends (aside from Lala, I couldn't claim any), and my new attitude (they claimed I had developed one) ached like a sore tooth. My mother's attempts to infuse holiday spirit into the visit only made it worse.

The lighting of the menorah emphasized the brevity of my visit, as I would be gone before all eight candles were lit. The silly things

I had loved as a child: the gilt dreidel that once belonged to my mother, the set of badly formed candles I had made in Hebrew school, and the moth-eaten stocking I had insisted we hang on the mantel when I was five, seemed small and sad. They were reminders of happier times, but they did not make me smile more or resent my parents' questions less. They only revealed how wide the chasm was between the past and the present, how unbridgeable.

"Tick tock, tick tock," Ben calls. I turn about to find him in my doorway, peering at me. I pat my jacket down, as if running an illegal-weapons search on myself. Nervous gesture. I don't want him to know that I was looking at airplane flight prices when I should have been doing a thousand other things.

"I'm ready," I say, and grab my briefcase.

He nods, as if agreeing. He does it all the time. Nods when people say things that don't call for recognition. It alarms me to realize I can recognize this and several other of his quirks. Has he learned my jacket-patting habit or does he merely see me do things without considering why?

We step outside into sunshine so bright I squint in pain. Damn. I forgot my sunglasses upstairs, just like yesterday.

"Landry is going to try to introduce the death penalty. Just you watch," Ben warns.

"He can't." Landry is poised to begin introducing his witnesses. The verdict is far from in. Only if we get a guilty verdict can he discuss sentencing.

"Watch. He'll try."

"Good luck to him," I say, aware that Judge Pullman will crush any attempt to introduce such premature discussions.

"I suppose you think that's okay?"

"What?"

"You think Landry ought to be able to soften the jury up now, for sentencing? Rather than wait until the case has been decided." His tone is dismissive.

"What? No! I meant that Pullman won't allow it." I quicken my pace, though I am perspiring. "When are you going to accept that I am not trying to sabotage this case?" My feet move faster, speed-walking now. "I work ninety-hour weeks and spend my free time reading ballistics reports and revising my cross-examination. I drink Maalox by day and wine by night. When will you be satisfied? When I'm lying in a hospital bed beside you being treated for an ulcer the size of Canada?" I have stopped on the sidewalk. Cars slow as they drive past, staring at me waving my briefcase and shouting at the older gentleman in front of me.

Ben's face grows red. His mouth opens but no words come out.

"You have it so goddamn easy. For you this is open-and-shut. Send a guy to the chair, no problem." I step forward. "I don't think humans should have the right to take away life, even a murderer's. You can call me crazy. Call me a stupid Yankee Jew liberal bitch, but do not *ever* call me disloyal or impugn my professional reputation."

I turn on my heel and stride forward, not looking behind to see if his jaw is still unhinged. I stare ahead, at the cupola of the courthouse where the clock shows that it's 1:25. I look down at my watch: 1:15.

My feet slow as Ben's tasseled loafers approach. It will not do for us to appear in court looking as though we just had a fight on Mulberry Street for the entire world to witness. What was the name of that Dr. Seuss book my mother used to read me? *And to Think That I Saw It on Mulberry Street*? Indeed.

"Goldberg." I turn. His tomato coloring has faded to salmon. He is panting, out of breath, as if he ran half a mile instead of hurrying a few steps. Is he going to keel over?

I stand, waiting for what's coming. Ben breathes in and out a few times, staring at me as if I might explode again. "I didn't mean to imply that you haven't worked hard on this case." Now it is time for my jaw to unhinge. "You have, and I know it hasn't been made any easier by my absence from the office." Of all the moments to go grateful, he has to choose now.

"I never partnered with anyone who didn't support capital punishment." He stares at the courthouse's columns as if they can explain why he got stuck with me. "Not on a capital case."

I nod. "We don't see eye to eye on a lot of things, and we never will. That's fine. But I can't stand having you look at me as if I'm less committed because of my views."

"Aren't you?" He said it. I didn't think he would. I shift my weight to my back foot and meet Ben's unblinking stare.

"No. If anything, I am more committed. I have something to prove that you don't. The job comes first." I sigh before adding, "After all, I can always sign Amnesty International petitions when I'm off duty."

His eyes widen but he doesn't say anything.

"We're going to be late," I say, gesturing toward the clock face. It reads 1:30.

"It doesn't keep proper time, you know."

"I know."

Landry begins the afternoon by introducing his first witness, Rufus Wellington. Rufus was at the club where Marcus Rhodes and Calvin Washington argued and where Calvin was overheard to tell Marcus he would "beat him down until his mama wouldn't recognize him" if he didn't stop talking trash about the Redskins. Marcus continued to belittle Calvin's favorite team, calling all their fans "faggots" until his friend Fred Johnson pulled him aside. He warned Marcus not to taunt Calvin because Calvin ran with a tough crew and had been known to send people who pissed him off to the emergency ward.

Rufus, dressed in a suit that bunches over his chest, raises his right hand and swears to tell the whole truth and nothing but the truth. We, the prosecution, maintain a healthy skepticism about this.

"Mr. Wellington, were you present at Club Bling on March twenty-fifth?"

"Yes."

"Did you witness a conversation between Mr. Washington and the deceased, Marcus Rhodes, at that time?"

"Yes." Rufus stares at Calvin. Calvin stares back, his mouth curved up at the corners. Is this his happy face?

"Could you describe that conversation?"

Rufus looks at Landry as if he holds a conductor's baton. "Calvin was talking about sports and Marcus interrupted to say that the Redskins . . . um, sucked." Ben looks at me with eyes that say, "This kid is reluctant to use the word 'suck'? Nice acting job."

"And how did Mr. Washington respond?" Landry will never say "defendant," will always refer to Calvin by name, in an attempt to humanize him.

"Calvin told Marcus he didn't know what he was talking about."

"Did Mr. Washington threaten the victim?"

"No." Rufus answers before Landry has finished the question.

"You earlier heard testimony from Mr. Fred Johnson that Calvin Washington threatened to beat Marcus Rhodes. Are you saying that this exchange did not take place?" Landry approaches the jury box as he speaks, pulling their attention toward him.

"No. Calvin never said that. He told Marcus to shut up, but he didn't say he'd hurt him or nothing."

"Are you certain?"

"Yeah."

"And how did this encounter end?"

With Marcus dead on an elementary-school classroom floor. That's how it ended.

"Marcus's homie pulled him away. He could see what a jerk Marcus was being, so he made him stop talking trash."

A small rustle in the court alerts me to the fact that Fred Johnson is probably manifesting displeasure at this interpretation of events. Judge Pullman bangs the gavel and reminds everyone that he will not tolerate any disruption in his court. His gray eyes burn a hole behind me. He urges Landry to continue with a "Please proceed, counselor."

"No further questions."

Rufus begins to rise so Ben stands and says, "Excuse me, Mr. Wellington. If you wouldn't mind?" He looks at the witness chair.

Pullman says, "Mr. Wellington, if you'll take your seat I believe the prosecution may have some questions for you." Ben nods to the judge and Landry waves his hand before him.

"Your witness," he says, attempting to regain control of the moment.

"Mr. Wellington, where were you when the defendant and the victim were having their . . . ah . . . discussion?" Ben's prevarication makes it clear that he wants to use a stronger word. It's better than if he used the word "fight," provoking Landry to object.

"At the bar."

"About how far away were you from the defendant and Mr. Rhodes?"

"I don't know. Close enough. I could hear everything."

"I see. What act was performing the night of March twenty-fifth?"

"Gangsta Nation." Rufus appears amused by the question.

"I see. And were they playing during this exchange?"

Rufus nods, prompting Pullman to instruct him to respond verbally. "Yes."

"And how would you characterize the volume level?"

"What?"

"I am curious as to how you would describe the noise level in the club during the conversation between the defendant and the victim."

"Oh. It was loud, but not real loud. I was close by, so I could hear everything."

Juror number three, Mrs. Little, wrinkles her nose. She does this when she suspects someone is pulling her leg. I had seen her do it before, during Fred's testimony. Nice to see that she applies the same standard to the defense.

"Mr. Wellington, would you be surprised to know that the police received five noise-complaint calls on the night of March twenty-fifth relating to the show at Club Bling that evening?"

The shoulders of his suit jacket strain as Rufus shrugs. "People complain about noise and stuff all the time. They probably just don't like that *style* of music."

"I see. So you didn't find the noise to be overwhelming? In fact you found it to be so low that you could overhear a conversation held within the club at a distance of several feet from you?"

"Yes." His vehement assertion holds the line, but jurors number five and seven are frowning. Sometimes the more inflexible a witness is, the more doubtful the jurors find him.

"No further questions." Ben did not discredit him, but he did raise doubt. We presented our version. They presented theirs.

"Counselor?" The judge looks to Landry, who rises and asks Rufus, "Mr. Wellington, are you at all hearing impaired?"

"No. My hearing always tested excellent."

The wrinkles that appear on Ben's face alert me to his desire to question these "tests" but he refrains, probably concluding that placing too much emphasis on them may credit Rufus's testimony more than we wish.

"Thank you, Mr. Wellington. That is all."

We decline to ask any further questions. Rufus steps down from the stand and walks away. Witness number one gone. I stare at Ben's sloped nose in profile and wonder how he thinks he did. Impossible to say, but I think he is pleased. He isn't clenching his pen like he does when he is upset. Dear God, you would think we were married, the way I have learned his mannerisms.

Landry calls his second witness, Loretta Dalton, a schoolteacher at Burke Elementary School and the last person known to have seen Marcus Rhodes besides his murderer. I sit a little straighter and watch a pale woman in a plaid print dress approach the witness box.

Her testimony seems irrelevant. Aside from characterizing Marcus Rhodes as a slack employee and confirming that she saw him cleaning at 5:25 P.M. on March 28 she offers little. She does mention that Marcus's regrettable tendency to not dust the classrooms could account for old fingerprints existing on doorframes. Is Landry serious? Does he actually believe the jury will swallow the notion that Calvin was in the school months or years earlier and that explains why his prints were found in that schoolroom?

Ms. Dalton is the final witness of the day. The late, elongated lunch pushed us into the afternoon and Judge Pullman assesses that it is unlikely we will get through the testimony and cross-examination of the next witness, Abraham Gentry. My stomach somersaults, relieved and distressed by the postponement of my courtroom duty. Ben and I exit the courtroom together and separate, by silent assent, at the corner. He walks west on Second and I head up Walnut, toward the office.

I stop at the office long enough to grab a handful of tampons from the stash I keep in my office. I don't want to stop at the drugstore. I head out, lowering my head, a charging bull, trying to discourage questions about how I am or how the case is proceeding. It works. No one asks me anything.

My briefcase seems to have gained weight, straining my arm as I ascend my driveway. While winding my way through the accumulating debris of the past week—telephone books to be recycled, clothes to be dry-cleaned, things I have used and not returned to their proper place—I am suddenly caught short. It looks a little like Ben's office.

"Shit," I mutter, dropping the briefcase, refusing to carry it an inch farther. I extract a tampon before heading to the bathroom, remembering that my towels need to be laundered.

The blinking light of my answering machine stops me. Check now or wait? I tap the tampon against my thigh and consider. What are the chances it is extraordinarily good news? I go to the bathroom.

When I reemerge I find myself staring at the pulsing red light, unwilling to depress the play button, to allow whatever is inside out. Pandora's box. I scold myself for being dramatic and reach forward.

"Natalie? It's Adam Griffon, from Harvard." My muscles relax. "I'm headed your way soon. I'm driving from a conference in Atlanta to a wedding in Savannah and I heard you had moved to Georgia so I called your parents." Oh, no, my mother will remember how well mannered Adam is and how Jewish. Damn. "They gave me your phone number. I hope you don't mind. Anyway, if you are free I would love to see you, maybe have dinner? I'm traveling with my girlfriend, Sonya. Sonya Patterson. She was a year below us. I'm not sure if you knew her." Oh, yes. The blonde with the slight lisp and the funny striped scarf she wore from September until May. "So if you're available we'd love to meet you. We expect to be in town on Saturday, the ah . . . twenty-third."

Adam recites three telephone numbers where he can be reached and wishes me a good week. Adam and Sonya. I would not have pictured them together. Sonya came from a hippie commune and Adam always wore a tie, perfectly knotted.

Into the kitchen to look at the calendar. Saturday the twenty-third is ten days away and I have no conflicting plans. The trial might be over by then. I grab a pen to make note of the numbers Adam left, resolving to call tomorrow to say I would be happy to meet him and Sonya for dinner. As the tape rewinds with a screech, I become conscious that not too long ago I would have invented an excuse to avoid meeting a former classmate.

Adam was a good friend, but after law school we lost touch. He will want to hear about New York and why I came to Macon. I will tell him I hated corporate law and wanted to explore criminal law and that it is fascinating. I will not tell him about Henry and the partners. As far as I am concerned they are no longer part of the story.

Chapter Twenty-six

September 14, 2000

Today is the day. I am cross-examining a witness. The training wheels are off. It is time to perform before the audience of friends and families of both the victims and the defendant, of newspaper reporters, of judge, jury, defense, and, most important, Ben.

Judge Pullman enters the room and the gentle swell of conversation ebbs into silence. Landry takes his witness, Mr. Abraham Gentry, through his testimony. The pale man seated in the witness box is the fifty-two-year-old factory employee who claims he saw Calvin Washington at the Columbus gas station at six-thirty P.M. on Tuesday, March 28. The murders happened around that time. The jury will not believe that our prime suspect was filling his gas tank while we claim he was killing two people. We must make them choose.

Landry walks Mr. Gentry through his sighting, asking him if the man he saw that evening is in the courtroom and then asking him to point to the man. Asking the court to please note that the witness gestured to the defendant, Mr. Calvin Washington. Calvin sits straight and silent, but his taut face appears to relax when Mr.

Gentry points to him. Landry asks Mr. Gentry if he is sure and Mr. Gentry says he is positive. The word "liar" appears in my head like a cartoon bubble before I can stop it from forming. I do not think he is lying. He believes that the man he saw at the gas station was Calvin Washington, but he is wrong.

Landry finishes, thanking Mr. Gentry for his service. Then he turns to Ben and me. "Your witness," he says with all the politeness of a person offering you sugar for your tea.

I rise on legs less sturdy than I prefer. I walk about the table's right side, my side, the side nearer the jurors. Bile rises in my throat; I swallow the bitter liquid. Stage fright, I get it something awful. I walk forward, breathing through my nose.

Standing before the witness box I shift my weight. Even in my heels the rail of the well-polished pine box reaches my breastbone. I must look like a miniadult to the jurors and courtroom spectators. Let them see me small. Let the witness think me little.

"Mr. Gentry, you said you saw Calvin Washington at the Sunoco gas station at six-thirty P.M. on March twenty-eighth?" My voice is soft, my tone gentle, apologetic for making him repeat himself.

"Yes."

"You are sure it was six-thirty P.M.?" Again I am gentle.

"Yes."

"May I ask how you knew it was six-thirty?" With this I turn to glance at Ben behind me, who sits, watching me as if I am about to throw the World Series, Bill Buckner style.

"I checked my watch a few minutes before I went to get the gas, and it was just before six-thirty."

I look back at Ben as if to say, "What next?" Letting Gentry think I am acting on Ben's command will make him regard me as less dangerous. I return my attention to Mr. Gentry. "And when did you see the defendant?"

"Six-thirty." Somebody titters.

"No, Mr. Gentry, I meant when, while you were at the gas station, did you see him? Was he there when you pulled up or did he drive in while you were pumping gas?"

"He was there when I pulled in." He is not offering more than I am asking. Landry and his team coached him well. Extraneous details are like shoelaces, easily tripped over.

"Inside or outside his car?"

"Outside, filling his tank."

I sigh, as if I wished he had answered differently. "And how long was he there?"

"He was still there when I drove off." Mr. Gentry crosses his legs, relaxing his rigid posture. He knows all the answers to my questions.

"And when did you leave the gas station?"

"About five minutes later. I filled up my tank, paid inside, and left. He"—Mr. Gentry nods toward Calvin Washington—"was still standing by his car when I left."

"I see. Did you recognize the car the defendant was driving?" I tilt my head, birdlike, inquisitive. Tell me all about cars, my gesture says.

Mr. Gentry responds to my feminine plea with a sheepish grin. "It was one of them new cars, the flashy ones. An Acura, I think. Red." Juror five's eyebrows are raised in what looks to be disbelief. Apparently he has trouble crediting a witness who cannot identify a car's make, model, and year on sight.

"Mr. Washington drives a 1999 Acura NSX." I walk back toward our table and withdraw a shiny photograph of the car from my folder. I submit it into evidence. "Mr. Gentry, is this the type of car you saw?"

He nods, relieved. He is still answering everything, still at the head of his class.

"It's a popular car," I say, turning to include the jury. A few sit straighter and watch me. This is part of the job. Making sure you do not lose their attention, keeping them focused. "In fact, it was one of the most popular cars sold in 1999. So lots of people own them."

Landry shifts in his seat, staring at me, not ready to insist that the judge make me make my point, but he is considering it. I save him the effort with my next question.

"Mr. Gentry, how many people, other than the defendant, were at the gas station that day?"

"Two."

"Two?"

"Two." He is confident again.

"Could you describe the two other people you saw at the gas station?"

"A man and a woman, in a truck."

"A man and a woman in a truck. What sort of truck?"

"Black." His predilection for describing cars by their color is causing juror five to twitch.

"A black truck. Did you notice the model?"

"It was a Chevy, I think."

"You think?"

"Yes. A Chevy. New."

"A new black Chevy." By stringing the words together slowly, like beads on a string, I reveal how empty they are, how lacking in substance. "What about the passengers? Could you describe them?"

"A man and a woman. She had sunglasses on."

"Were they inside the truck?"

"No, they were outside, pumping gas."

"Both of them?"

"He was. She wasn't. She was just standing there."

"And did you notice their clothes, other than the sunglasses?"

"Blue jeans. And a T-shirt. And sneakers, or boots."

"Both of them?"

He hesitates. "Yeah."

I manage to swing a "what woman dresses like her companion?" look toward the jury. No matter that many women wear jeans and T-shirts. It just sounds so convenient for this couple to be dressed as twins.

"And Mr. Washington? How was he dressed?" For once I do not refer to him as the defendant.

"He had long shorts and a basketball jersey. Black and red. It was a Chicago Bulls shirt, number twenty-three, and high-top sneakers."

"A Michael Jordan Chicago Bulls basketball jersey atop long shorts, with sneakers. That is quite a description. May I ask why you are able to recall Mr. Washington's attire so clearly when you seem less specific about the mystery couple's outfits?"

"Objection," Landry interjects. "The prosecution's reference to a mystery couple is uncalled for."

"Sustained," the judge responds. "Miss Goldberg, please watch your use of adjectives."

"Yes, Your Honor." The jurors won't forget what I said.

"Mr. Gentry, why did Mr. Washington's attire make such an impression on you?"

"He seemed more noticeable." Mr. Gentry shifts in his seat, his movement more squirming than settling down.

Because he was a young black man? Possibly. However, I need to show Gentry's memory is specific because it is based on another image, a different memory.

"Mr. Gentry, you have stated that you saw only a man and a woman besides the defendant at the gas station. What about the sales clerk? Did you forget to pay for your gas?"

"Oh, him. Yeah, I saw the clerk, too. Young kid. He's there most evenings."

"And yet he didn't recall seeing the defendant."

"He probably sees a lot of people, and can't remember them all." Mr. Gentry sits a bit straighter.

"I see. Mr. Gentry, when did you notify the police that you had seen Mr. Washington at the gas station?"

"On March thirty-first."

"And what prompted you to telephone the police?" I look out the windows, implying that his answer doesn't mean much.

"I saw a news clip that showed that he"—Mr. Gentry nods toward Calvin—"had been arrested for murder. I heard the anchorman say that the murder had taken place on the evening of March twenty-eighth. I realized I had seen him that evening, so I telephoned them."

"Did the news account say when the murder had taken place?" I am skating atop a knife's edge here. It is important to help him out so that I can crush him. Tricky.

"No, just that it happened on the evening of the twenty-eighth."

"So when you telephoned the police you had no idea what sort of information you were providing?"

Some of the jurors shift, their faces scrunched in thought. Good.

"Pardon?" Mr. Gentry cannot foresee where I am headed, either.

"I am sorry," I say, offering a small smile. "What I mean is that when you called the police to inform them that you had seen the defendant at the gas station in Columbus, you did not know that you were providing him with an alibi for the time of the murders. Is that correct?"

"Yes," he affirms. For all he knew, he had spotted the murderer fleeing the scene of the crime. Only he did not. He did not see the murderer until today.

I have established that Mr. Gentry did not seek to acquit Mr. Washington of a crime, increasing his witness credibility. Time to destroy that.

"Mr. Gentry, when you saw the person you have identified as the defendant did you notice anything particular about him aside from his clothing?"

Mr. Gentry frowns. Damn. I need him to say it. He did before, in the report, but I cannot put the words in his mouth.

"No."

"You did not notice anything about him while he was pumping gas?" I fight the urge to pantomime the act of pumping gas, to trigger his memory.

"Oh, his hand was bandaged," Mr. Gentry says. He sits back a little.

I resist the urge to throw a triumphant smile at Ben. I say quietly, "His hand was bandaged. Can you recall which hand?"

Landry has moved in his seat. He knows what is coming, and he cannot do anything to stop it. His train just jumped the tracks and now he has to watch it crash.

"His left hand."

"With gauze?"

"Yes."

"Mr. Gentry, when you saw Mr. Washington on television did you happen to notice if his hand was bandaged?"

"Yes, it was. They showed him being led into the police station, in handcuffs, and you could see his hands behind him. The left was bandaged in gauze."

"I see. Mr. Washington's hand was bandaged as he was led into the police station. According to Mr. Washington, he injured his hand repairing a friend's door frame that very day." This to explain the wooden splinters found in his hand that we maintain came from wielding a bat at Marcus Rhodes. "What is odd is that neither of Mr. Washington's hands was bandaged when the police arrived." I approach the witness box, so close I can see Mr. Gentry's hands clutch each other.

"And no gauze was found at Mr. Washington's residence. You see, one of the policemen bandaged Mr. Washington's hand. It had begun to bleed." It began bleeding when he attempted to strike one of the police officers, or so Detective Wilkins told me. "The police bandaged it.

"So you see, Mr. Gentry, until the evening of March thirty-first Calvin Washington was not wearing a gauze bandage on his left hand. Are you sure he was wearing one at the gas station?" My tone holds pity, as if I am trying to offer him a way out.

"No. Wait, yes." This reversal causes several people to lean forward closer. They are sharks, and the scent of blood on the water is unmistakable.

"Which is it, Mr. Gentry?"

"Yes, I saw the bandage." His face quivers like that of a rabbit. "He could have worn it then and lost it or taken it off later."

"Except that no one who saw Calvin Washington from March twenty-eighth to March thirty-first has mentioned that bandage, Mr. Gentry. No one but you. Until it appeared on the eleven o'clock news no one but members of the Macon Police Department saw it." My voice is laden with conviction. You are wrong, I say with every syllable. Wrong, wrong, wrong.

"Mr. Gentry, is it possible that the man you saw at the gas station on March twenty-eighth was not the defendant, but someone else? Someone who was wearing a bandage and the sight of that bandage on the news triggered a recollection?"

"I . . . I don't know," he concludes. He looks to Landry as if he can help him, but he can't.

"I have no further questions." Before I have reached my seat Landry is standing and asking, "Mr. Gentry, did anyone ask that you identify Mr. Washington?"

Mr. Gentry tilts his head to one side. "Pardon?"

Landry clears his throat before saying, "Mr. Gentry, no one asked that you identify Mr. Washington"—Landry gestures toward his client—"did they? No one from my office contacted you?"

"No," Mr. Gentry says, sitting straighter. "No, sir. I simply called the police after I saw the news piece."

Idiot, I think, as Landry thanks Mr. Gentry. Landry just fumbled in the worst way. By implying that Mr. Gentry could have been sought by the defense he introduced a previously foreign suspicion into the jurors' minds and did nothing but reinforce the fact that Gentry's identification was based on the television coverage, our point exactly.

When Pullman asks if I have anything further I rise from my seat. "Mr. Gentry, did you happen to notice what Mr. Washington was wearing on the news broadcast when he was arrested?"

Gentry squirms like a worm on a hook. "Um, shorts and a shirt."

"Could you be more specific?"

"Denim shorts and a basketball jersey." His voice quivers.

"I see. No further questions." We're done.

I sit and allow myself a quick glance at Ben. He stares ahead as Landry hurries to call his next witness, a medical expert who will attempt to downplay the importance of the blood found on Calvin Washington's clothes.

It is difficult to sit still. I am juiced full of adrenaline. I look down and notice a small mark on my pad of paper. "Good job" it reads. Ben wrote it. My face twitches with the effort of repressing a smile. This is the biggest check-plus of my life, the largest compliment ever received. Better than any A on a paper, better than passing the bar, better than all of Henry's *I love yous.*

I look up, intent on concentrating on Landry's efforts to reconstruct his case. We are going to win. I know it. We have taken reasonable doubt away. We are going to win.

Chapter Twenty-seven

September 19, 2000

Despite my machine's autobrew feature I scorched the coffee this morning. I spent four minutes brushing the charred taste from my mouth. When I left the house I found that raccoons had invaded my trashcan, leaving a trail of garbage along my driveway. Now my panty hose have snagged on my chair.

I feel behind my leg. Damn. The hole is even bigger than I thought. Ben catches me squirming.

"Goldberg, what are you doing?"

"I need to go to the bathroom. I have a hole in my panty hose."

"No one cares about your panty hose."

"I care." I don't want to face the verdict of my first murder trial in torn panty hose.

"Pullman is going to return any minute," he warns.

"It will only take a minute. I have a spare pair in my briefcase."

Ben raises his eyebrows, but I sense he is not surprised. "Go then, but make it quick."

The bailiff stands to attention and I hesitate, but Ben says, "Go!

If Pullman comes I'll tell him you had to visit the ladies' room. He's used to nervous preemies."

I hurry to the restroom. "Preemies," the slang term for new lawyers. I wonder when I will stop being a preemie. I enter a stall, remove my torn hose, extract the new pair, and struggle into them with several muttered oaths. I emerge from the bathroom a little out of breath and red in the face.

When I return to the courtroom Pullman is there, seated. He looks at me, but does not say a word. His stare is enough.

"All better?" Ben asks.

Landry calls his last witness, Dr. Moran, a forensics expert who testifies that the wood splinters found in Washington's hand and clothes and car might not have come from the baseball bat used to beat Marcus Rhodes. Dr. Moran wears bifocals and a toupee and has the voice of a child. Several times Judge Pullman has to ask him to speak up or repeat his answer. The jurors frown at him or smile, amused. I hope Landry did not pay much for his expertise.

After Landry finishes, Ben asks the witness a few questions, managing, with a few well-placed modifiers, to make Dr. Moran retract nearly everything he has said. Landry does not reexamine. The defense rests. I glance at my watch. It's 10:07 A.M.

The closing arguments begin. Ben reminds the jury of the damning evidence they have heard. He tells them that this is not only about determining guilt or innocence: it is about justice. Justice for the dead—Marcus Rhodes and Dominic Brown—and justice for their family members. At this, Emily Brown sobs, just loudly enough to carry to the jury box. She could not have timed it better.

Landry adjusts his glasses before rising to give his speech. "Ladies and gentlemen, you have heard my esteemed colleague speak of justice. Justice is what we should keep foremost in our mind.

Justice for all. My client too deserves your justice. Our criminal trial decisions are predicated on the concept of reasonable doubt. Surely, you have heard of several instances in which this applies. Has the prosecution managed to find the actual instrument that killed both Mr. Rhodes and Dominic Brown? Have they discovered that gun or connected it to my client? They have not. Have they shown that the discussion between my client and Mr. Rhodes is the stuff of which murders are made? Have they proven that no one but my client, Mr. Washington, could have committed this crime?"

He continues in this vein for some time and concludes with a hope that the jurors will keep the word "justice" in their minds during their deliberations. I glance at my watch: 10:32.

Judge Pullman instructs the jury. He is thorough in his explanations. He excuses them to deliberate at 11:01. Court is adjourned until the jurors reach their verdict.

"Come on," Ben says. "Let's go back to the office." He reads my face. "They'll call us when they are ready."

On the way, we talk about the weather. It is so hot Ben mops his brow with his handkerchief three times during the trip. I feel full of tension and humming awareness, like a springboard platform awaiting the feet of a diver.

Once inside Ben tells me, "Be ready."

I resolve not to go farther than the restroom.

Today the offices are quiet, with fewer phones ringing. I nod hello to the secretaries, notice that the toner seems to be low on the copy machine, and that the water is almost gone from the cooler again. I will have to hurry if I want to get a cup. Carl is coerced into hauling another five-gallon bottle atop the cooler most often. He never says no.

Speak of the devil, I think. Several yards off, Carl huddles over the desk of our newest intern. "Desk" may be too glorified a term as the intern is working at a small typing table we used to rest copier paper on. Carl is explaining scheduling trial dates and judge rotations, pointing with his forefinger to boxed dates on a calendar. His voice is low and patient. Passing by, I realize that something is off. Slowing my steps, I look back over my shoulder. Carl isn't twitching, tapping, or pacing.

Standing in front of my office's air-conditioning unit, I consider this. Have I seen Carl tap his pencil against his teeth when he talks to Ben? Not that I remember. What about with Will? Does he shuffle his feet or play with his paper clips? No, I saw them talking by the elevator last week and Carl seemed fine.

The ideas taking shape in my mind both fascinate and terrify me. Where have I been this past year? Am I really that unaware, that blind? Yes. Yes. So wrapped up in my escape from New York, my anger at Henry, studying for the bar, and my introduction to Macon that I noticed little around me. Too wrapped up in the drama of my own trial—*World v. Natalie Goldberg*—that I did not see what everyone else must. Carl is only nervous when around me. I try to stop the smile from forming but I cannot.

Once the air conditioner has cooled me to room temperature I concentrate on my in box. My own paper Tower of Pisa, ready to topple any second. Sorting the pending cases and the calls from defense attorneys looking to wheel and deal occupies me until one-thirty when my rumbling stomach alerts me to the fact that it has not consumed anything since a breakfast of burned coffee and yogurt. I cannot predict when we will be called back to court, but better safe than hungry. I speed-dial Atlanta Bread Company for some soup and salad.

I have consumed a third of it when Ben stops outside my office. He carries his worn briefcase in his hand. I think he cannot be here to tell me what he says next. "They're ready."

A chunk of tomato dangles on my plastic fork. It moves a bit, as my hand shakes.

"So soon?" I say. It is 2:19. They have deliberated less than three hours.

He nods. I trash my lunch and gather my things, fumbling with my bag.

Ben tells me I have time to visit the washroom if I like, for which I am grateful. I check my panty hose twice. Then I reapply my lipstick and exhale several times. At least I don't feel nauseous.

Ben seems sure that such a short deliberation means we have won it. I think we should have, but worry all the same. What if the jury was swayed by Landry's rhetoric?

The courtroom buzzes with speculation. I overhear two reporters laying odds on the verdict.

The bailiff announces court is in session and we rise for Judge Pullman. He silences the whisperers with a request that all talking cease and that the jury be brought in. They come, single file, eyes ahead. Judge Pullman asks if they have reached a verdict. Mr. Jerison, the quiet, bespectacled man who serves as foreman, says they have. Pullman asks, "In the matter of the charge of first-degree murder of Marcus Rhodes, how do you find?"

Mr. Jerison pushes his glasses higher up on his nose and then reads in a strong voice, "We the jury find the defendant, Calvin Washington, guilty." A few people inhale sharply. Others sigh, as if relieved. A woman moans; I assume it is Calvin's sister. Judge Pullman asks Mr. Jerison to continue. He does. The jury finds Calvin Washington guilty of the murder of Dominic Brown.

Ben's hands tighten into fists. He does not smile, but I know he is happy. We got him. The jury did not buy the "where is the gun" diversion or Landry's attempt to make it seem the police railroaded Calvin.

"We will begin the sentencing hearing tomorrow morning at eight o'clock. Until then, members of the jury, you have my thanks for your careful work." Pullman nods at the jurors and then rises.

I stand. Ben stands. We smile at each other. Then the Browns, always seated behind us, call our names. Emily hugs each of us. "Thank you," she and her husband say. "Thank you."

Ben squeezes her slender hands between his own and says, "I am sure Dominic is watching in heaven right now. May peace be with you."

Then it is time for the Rhodeses to approach us. I have seen Marcus's mother, father, and brother in court. They have alternated, as if taking shifts, but today all three are present and all three give us their thanks. Tears slide down Mrs. Rhodes's round cheeks. Ben speaks to them, wishing them success in putting this behind them.

I follow Ben outside into a waiting throng of reporters. Camera bulbs blind me. Ben has no trouble. He smiles and says the jury did extraordinary work and that he is satisfied to have removed a dangerous killer from the community. After he finishes, questions are shouted at him. One aggressive redhead shoves a microphone under my mouth and asks how I feel about tomorrow's sentencing hearing and do I think we will get the death penalty? How to answer? I cannot say "I hope not," so I say I cannot predict the outcome and that I can only hope for the best.

We take a cab back to the office, seeking relief from the humidity-soaked air. "We did it," Ben says. He turns so that he is facing me. "You did good work. Handled Gentry like a pro."

"Thank you." I am tempted to look outside the cab window for flying pigs.

"Let's go tell Will."

Will is locked behind his heavy oak door but he emerges from his cool office to hear our story. "Congratulations," he says. "Tomorrow is sentencing? I'll be out of the office, paying my respects to the governor and his inner circle, but keep me informed."

The news of our victory spreads. As we walk the halls others call out their congratulations. How very different from Walters, MacLittle, and Tate, where achievements were viewed by colleagues with envy or skepticism.

"Do you need help with tomorrow's statement?" I ask Ben.

He shrugs. "Nothing has changed. It's more Landry's show than ours." Landry has to persuade the jury that there were mitigating factors that compelled his client to act as he did.

"Go work on your other cases," he says. "Day is almost over anyway." It's 4:10, but since when do we keep normal hours?

In my office I try to return to the tasks I left unfinished but concentration eludes me. My clothes still smell of the scent Emily Brown wears, something with lavender in it. My mind jumps to tomorrow's outcome. Will they decide to send him to the chair? My throat tightens. "It's out of your hands," I tell myself. "Your job is done."

At 4:32 Carl knocks on my door. "Hey, Nat, I heard about your win. Congratulations."

"Thanks. Most credit is due to Ben."

He rubs his jaw, which has no five o'clock shadow. Huh. I have never seen Carl with facial hair. Either he shaves three times a day or he does not grow it much. Another thing I have never thought about.

"Come on in. I can't think."

"Wired?" he asks, sitting down.

"A little." The energy that has been coursing through me ever since the word "guilty" was spoken has settled to a low-pitched hum, but I can still feel it.

"It will pass," he predicts. "When it does, you'll be exhausted.

Probably sleep better than you have in weeks." Is he blushing? Or are his cheeks just that shade?

"I could use it."

He glances at my desk, at my multiple "to do" lists and color-coded file folders. He straightens his tie, although it is already straight.

"How is Sarah?" I ask.

"Good. I wanted to tell you she is looking for a job. She suspects that once the divorce goes through William will drag his feet on anteing up alimony or child support."

"That's what the courts are for."

He looks at my paper clip collection. I wait, counting mentally. One, two, three, four, five, six. He begins drumming his fingers against his leg. Aha!

"Sentencing is tomorrow?"

"Yes." Talk of tomorrow makes me queasy.

He drums his fingers a little faster.

"Everything okay?" I ask. He looks up. My, his eyes are blue.

"Sure, why?"

"Well, you're sort of fidgeting." His fingers are halfway through their up-and-down cycle.

"Oh. No, I'm just . . . I'll stop." He does.

"Come to think of it, Carl, I've noticed you tend to fidget."

"Me?"

"Yes. I notice you only seem to do it around me, though."

"Am I being cross-examined?" he asks. Now he is pulling at the handkerchief in his breast pocket. He is going to ruin its perfect triangle point.

"No, I'm sorry. I just hope I don't make you nervous." This is not the truth, but it sounds good.

"No, you—" He sighs. His eyes are the color of hydrangeas.

"You don't. Really. It's me. I just—I like you, Natalie. A lot." He sounds anguished.

"Okay." I am trying not to blush.

"I just don't want to compromise our working relationship, so I'm sorry I mentioned it and you can forget it."

"Can I?" This is not the sort of thing you forget. I know. I tried not to desire Henry. Look how well that turned out.

"Can't you?"

"I don't know," I tell him. We stare at each other for a few moments, and then look away. I contemplate turning the air conditioner to high.

"I have a court case tomorrow, so I better start preparing," he says. I wonder whether this is true, and then decide that Carl's faults don't include lying.

"Good luck," I say.

After he leaves I stand in front of the air conditioner and let the air flutter the sleeves of my silk blouse. When was the last time I felt hot in the face like this? Oh, yes, this morning, after changing my panty hose, on my rush back to the courtroom. Somehow our victory seems distant, as if it occurred days, and not hours, ago.

I think about tomorrow. My stomach gurgles. Carl was a terrific distraction from the sentencing of Calvin Washington, but now my brain has remembered and it has alerted my body. I wonder if it is the cool air or if it is fear causing the goose bumps to rise on my skin.

Chapter Twenty-eight

September 22, 2000

Where is the damn rice cereal? Rows of cereal line the shelves of aisle 3, a cardboard land of plenty, but can I find the one box I want? I glare at cartoon rabbits and leprechauns as if they are responsible for my missing cereal. Aha, there it is! Holding the middle ground between the land of the sugar laden and the land of the fiber rich. I toss the box into my shopping cart, atop several containers of yogurt and a bottle of orange juice.

The cart's right front wheel squeaks as I push forward toward the promise of bread products. My pursuit of carbohydrates recalls a conversation I had with Lacey last weekend in which she told me that her uncle was on the Atkins diet. "As much bacon as he wants but no bread or sugar. I don't care what they say about man can't live by bread alone. I can," she insisted. "Especially if it has cinnamon sugar on top." I wonder if Lacey's boyfriend has noticed she has the gastrointestinal strength of a goat. Tom? No, Todd. God, don't let me screw that up when I meet him. I'm getting as bad as my father with names.

He called last night. When I did not get out of bed to answer the phone he left a message. "Nat? Are you there? It's Dad. I heard about your case. I wanted to see how you are. Give me a call when you get a chance, princess."

He knew we had won the case and he knew what it meant. He might have predicted my reaction to Calvin Washington's death sentence: vomiting until my stomach was empty. His voice on the message, inquisitive, almost fearful, said it all. My God, he had not called me "princess" since I told him about Henry.

I reach for the saltines, resolving to combine them with ginger ale. My stomach has not settled completely. After this morning's breakfast of toast and tea I rushed to the bathroom to find the seasick heaving had subsided, but it was a close call. I grab a loaf of wheat bread, checking the sell date. My cart's squeaky wheel protests my efforts to steer it around the corner to aisle 5, Canned Vegetables, Fruits, and Soups.

Chicken soup sounds good. I put three cans in the bottom of the cart, careful not to crush the bread or crackers. Up the aisle, past the harried mother of three whose hair needs cutting, to the canned fruit. I have a weakness for canned fruit salad. "White trashtastic" Lacey would say, but I don't care. It is comfort food and I need comfort.

When the jurors had reentered the courtroom, shuffling, eyes averted, my stomach clenched. I wondered if the eyes they were avoiding were each other's. If they could not come to agreement, Calvin Washington could not be sentenced to death. In Georgia, if just one juror holds out, the death penalty cannot be imposed.

Mr. Jerison read from a sheet of paper that moved in his quaking hands. His voice sounded robotic. He said that the jury had found for sentencing Calvin Washington to death. Emily Brown hiccupped behind me. Calvin moved in his chair, drawing the bailiffs forward, but no restraint needed to be applied. Landry grimaced, his boyish face aged by disappointment. The jury members stared ahead, looking like flu survivors, weary and wanting their beds.

Did I move or stir or make a sound? I don't know. Pullman remanded Washington to the Georgia Diagnostic and Classification Prison. He told him, "What you have done is irrevocable. The harm you have inflicted cannot be undone, and now you will face the consequences of your actions. May God have mercy on your soul." Calvin's sister, Donna, and cousin, Toya, sobbed into fistfuls of tissues. Then Pullman thanked the jurors and they rose, aged two decades since entering the courtroom two weeks ago.

Ben turned to me and said only, "We're done."

"Excuse me," the mother of three says. Behind her, two of her kids argue over who gets to hold the box of cookies.

"Sorry," I apologize, stepping back so that she can grab two cans of cling peaches. The children are yelling "Give it to me, it's my turn!" as I walk past them.

In the produce section I stare at a pile of tomatoes. They are stacked precariously; one false move will topple the pyramid. Sort of like Ben's office. Ben. After the trial he spoke to the press and made hearty about the verdict and the sentence, giving the jurors credit for an "incredibly difficult task." I caught the end of his speech, after my vomiting subsided. He did not say anything about my sudden departure to the restroom. He did not ask if I was okay. He could see that I was not.

I touch the topmost tomato, stroking its delicate, silky skin. So vulnerable to bruising, so easily spoiled. I pick it up, carefully, and transfer it to a clear produce bag and place it in the front of the cart.

My food purchases fill six brown paper bags. When will I eat it all?

After I have unloaded the groceries into the trunk, my car sits lower. The backseat contains bags of clothes to be donated to Goodwill along with household items Lala asked me to drop off when I mentioned my impending visit. I turn on the radio just in time to catch the weather update. Seventy-eight degrees and sunny. A perfect day for playing hooky, though I am not. Will gave me the day off.

He came into my office yesterday afternoon, closing the door behind him. His gaze settled on the photographs of my father and me taken outside Harvard Yard. I had hung the pictures earlier that morning, bruising my thumb with a misplaced hammer blow. His gaze returned to me as he sat.

"Hello, Will," I said, because he seemed disinclined to start.

He templed his fingers. "I'm sorry I missed you yesterday. You and Ben did a wonderful job." His stress on the adjective was subtle, but I caught it. Wonderful.

"Thanks."

He stared nearsightedly at my photographs. "You're decorating." He sounded surprised.

"Yes, I thought it time." Along with the photographs and diplomas I had added a small potted fuchsia to the windowsill nearest the desk.

"So you're not planning to leave?" He sat back and crossed his legs.

My smile acknowledged his relief. "I would like to stay." Perhaps I could install a small table by the closet door, something less masculine, less Guvnor in style?

"I know it was tough yesterday. I thought you might decide this wasn't for you." Ben must have said something to Will.

I rubbed at the faint hammering that had begun behind my right temple. Recalling the moment when the verdict was read, when the word "death" sank into my brain and rippled outward, made my head hurt.

"I believe in the work we do here," I said, leaning forward to rest my elbows on the desk. Its solidity made me feel more secure. "But I don't ever want to prosecute another capital case again."

He uncrossed and recrossed his legs. "I thought you might say that . . ."

My torso felt as if it was being squeezed too tight. Here it comes, I thought. He will not keep me on, cannot let me continue if I will not play this part of the game.

"We need to get someone in here to replace Jeffrey. It's well past time. Unfortunately, Harvard-educated sharks don't swim downstream here all that often." His weary smile prompted one of my own. "I cannot guarantee that we will not have to come to you for another capital case again, but this is only the third such trial we have ever prosecuted during the past thirty years. The chances are very slim."

He looked at me and I knew he saw the purple shadows underneath my eyes. "You should take tomorrow off," he advised.

"Okay." His eyebrows leaped at my quick acceptance. "Oh, and Will, do you remember discussing my taking some vacation time?" Difficult to believe that conversation took place only three months ago.

"Of course. Do you have something planned?" He rose from his seat, ready to resume his other duties.

"I thought I might visit my parents in early November. I'll check the court schedules and talk to the others." I doubted Ben or Carl would object.

"I'm glad you're staying."

"Me, too. Oh, and thanks for not assuming I was some sort of ACLU undercover agent." I remembered Helen's comments about the suspicions regarding my motives for coming here.

Will's laughter oozed out of him, thick and deep. "I never thought you were. I just assumed you were crazy, like the rest of us." He winked at me before going.

The man behind the cracked linoleum counter at Goodwill eyes the two bottled ships Lala gave me to donate as if he expects them to explode. I push them closer and heft the three bags of clothing onto the counter, not giving him time to object. The clerk hands me a tax-deduction form. Then he shifts the clothes bags onto the crowded and not quite clean floor. When I exit the swinging door into the afternoon sun he still has not touched the model ships imprisoned in glass.

Prison. That is where Calvin Washington is now. In Georgia Diagnostic and Classification Prison in Jackson, wearing a white uniform with STATE PRISONER printed on the back. Where he will live while appeals are filed, if he can find a lawyer to write them. The three habeas corpus appeals allowed death-row prisoners must show that the defendant's fundamental rights were violated during the trial or the sentencing. Composing them is an involved process, so finding a lawyer to do so is no easy task. Who knows? Maybe Calvin will find someone like Stephen Bright, of the Southern Center for Human Rights, who will move heaven and earth to get his sentence commuted, but the odds are slim.

It is more likely that years from now Calvin Washington will consume his last meal. Then his scalp and right leg will be shaved free of hair. He will wear a diaper under his jumpsuit as the guards escort him to the room where the electric chair waits. A leather flap will be placed over his face, hiding it from the witnesses present to observe his last moments.

In the room behind him, a box with three wires will await three prison staff. Each will press the button. The wires are braided together so that they will not know which of them pushed the kill button. As if that can ease their guilt.

For four seconds after the button is pressed 1,800 volts will penetrate his skull through the electrode on his forehead. A 900-volt cycle lasting seven seconds will stun his heart, lungs, and kidneys. A third 300-volt cycle will make his heart's fibers quiver for 109 seconds, forcing the muscle to shut down. It is supposed to take two minutes to die in Georgia's electric chair. It has taken longer. Calvin does not seem the type to go easily.

My kitchen looks as though raccoons have run through it. Containers of food lie about, emptied from the cabinets so that I could clean inside this morning. I settle the bags of groceries atop any clear space on the table. Stacking cans of soup upon newly cleaned shelves, I remember my mother doing the same. She would place cans any which way, not concerned whether the label was visible. I used to rearrange them, turning them face out and aligning them just so. She laughed when she opened the cupboards. "Aaron, Nat's been at it again," she would tell my father. "I think we are the only parents on the block with a child who rearranges soup cans." She made it sound like a compliment, not a disorder.

The cans sit straight ahead, labels out. I rotate one a half-inch to the right, just to see. After five seconds my hand reaches to straighten it. The brown paper bags rustle as I fold them and put them in the now mostly empty recycling bin. Not bad for a half-day of cleaning.

I decide to place the phone call I avoided all morning. The phone rings three times before it is answered with a bright "hello."

"Hi, Mom." I settle into my corduroy seat cushion, my knees bumping the chair's arms.

"Natalie!" Her shout must have reached the neighbors. I hold the phone out from my ear. "Aaron, it's Natalie!" I'm made happy by my decision to extend the phone. The possibility of hearing loss is acute.

"Mom, I—" A click and then, "Natalie?" My father has picked up the study phone or the upstairs line.

"Honey, she's on the line," my mother explains.

"I don't hear her," my father complains.

"I'm here, Dad." They squawk at each other like temperamental parrots.

"Nattie, how are you?" he asks before my mother can echo, "Yes, sweetie, *how* are you? Your father is convinced you're not feeling well. He has been stalking the phone."

"Now, that's not true," he says. "I've just been hoping she would call."

"Pacing by it, actually," my mother continues.

"I'm okay. I took the day off. Actually, Will, the DA, gave it to me."

"Wasn't that nice?" my mother remarks.

"Yes, very," I reply, unable to keep the dryness from my voice. "And we talked about my work. I'm going to stay on." I exhale and the stomach jitters that settled hours ago begin quaking anew.

"You're okay?" He doesn't remark on my staying.

"After throwing up for several hours, yes, Dad, I'm fine." His half sigh, half harrumph resonates more than my mother's anxious cries about my intestinal trouble. Have I been able to keep anything down? she demands. I should try some crackers with a little ginger ale. My assurance that I bought both sends her to exclaiming that I shouldn't have to perform this task for myself and isn't there someone who could run these errands for me?

I assure her that I am capable of grocery shopping, but the scroll of names that appears in my head at my mother's question surprises me. Carl. Helen. Lala. Any of them would fetch me crackers. And there are more cracker fetchers in my future, I suspect. More friends to make, more people to stop pushing away.

"And a little broth," she concludes. I blink myself back to her voice.

"Thanks, Mom." I am unsure what advice I have just sanctioned.

"Do you think you'll visit anytime soon?" My father tries to keep the anxiety from his voice. He is worried, and with reason. He knows how it goes with me. The throwing up, the exhaustion, the nightmares. He is my father and he has held my curls from my face as I heaved over the toilet after taking my SATs. What is that compared to sending a man to the chair? This pain, then, is enough to earn forgiveness, whereas my heartache over Henry was not. My father's love is a complicated thing.

"Yes. I spoke to Will about taking some time in early November." My mother makes a loud, high sound of delight. "I thought I would visit Lacey in New York and then come home for a few days."

My parents' voices overlap as they discuss what we will do and how nice it will be to see me and did I know that Gerard Manowitz is in rehab? As if I need to know all the neighborhood gossip prior to my arrival, lest I unwittingly make a drug rehab joke before the Manowitzes.

"Okay, well, I just wanted to check in." I try to extract myself from the debate about whether Gerard was addicted to cocaine or pain medication. Mom holds out for the pain pills, Dad for the cocaine. I would lay money on cocaine. Gerard wasn't the pain-pill type and it sounds more like my mother trying to excuse his addiction on the grounds of a medical basis, improving his condition with some creative remembering.

"I'll talk to you soon," I say.

"Yes, okay," Mom says. "We love you, honey. Remember, ginger ale and crackers and maybe a heating pad."

"Take care, Nattie. I love you," Dad murmurs.

"Love you, too." My hand is slow to set the phone down, to release the flow of love. It was as before, when they would call and talk at once and I would only understand half of the conversation. I mustn't expect it to be this way. My parents' disappointment that I will remain here made their joy at my impending visit more buoyant. They want me home, but it isn't home any longer, or it is, but not my current home. I sigh and lever myself out of the chair. I still have things to do, on my day off.

Chapter Twenty-nine

September 23, 2000

The rose-patterned sheets, tangled from my restless sleep, cover half of my body. I move my head to rest flat on the pillow. Morning comes, the air weighty and damp, the sounds outside the window muffled. My pillow smells of toothpaste. I try to burrow deeper into the bedding, into myself, wrapping my left arm about my middle, my fingertips resting just by the scoop of my navel. My skin is soft and I smile. Sometimes the world is a dream from which I do not want to be woken.

Birdsong, loud and screechy, wakes me. Damn jays. They love Lala's garden. Groaning and rubbing my nose into the pillow, I curse the birds. What time is it anyway? The digital numbers of the bedside alarm shock me. Ten-thirty. When was the last morning I awoke later than nine? I cannot recall. Even on weekends my body cannot lie still after the sun has crossed the windowpanes to make a checkerboard pattern on my bed.

My limbs protest, still full of silty sleep, as I rise from bed and stretch. Oomph. The girl in the mirror is a fright, but she looks better than the girl of yesterday. The shadows beneath my eyes have paled and the darkness in the pupils has waned. My ears still ring with Landry's pleas for the jurors to have mercy upon Calvin Washington, but his voice has quieted.

I shuffle into the kitchen for coffee and toast. Perhaps I will have a banana, too. A bright pink sheet of paper hangs suspended by three magnets on my freezer, just above eye level, my long to-do list. While the coffeemaker chirps and coughs scented steam I reread the list, figuring out what tasks to handle today. I decide on the library, where I must return overdue books, and the dry cleaners where both pickup and drop-off is in order. I also promised Lala I would visit the garden-supply store and get some bulbs and potting soil for her. The coffeemaker gasps its last and I hurry to transfer some of the black liquid into my mug. No sugar, no milk, just unadulterated caffeine.

The moist air warns of a thunderstorm. Back home they would refer to this as an Indian summer day. Here we just call it September. The buttons on my shorts slip through their slots too easily. I have lost weight. A few honest-to-goodness meals and some ice cream ought to remedy that quick enough.

Adam and Sonya are coming today. I am taking them to Michael's on Mulberry. It was that or Hooters. I smile at my own joke, imagining their horror. Whenever Lacey complains that I have relocated to the middle of nowhere I am quick to observe that I live in a city where there is both a Hooters restaurant and Nu-Way Weiners and what has New York got to top these delightful establishments? She always gasps, amused and appalled.

I am surprised to see the glowing button on my answering machine. Did I sleep through a phone call? I press play.

"Natalie? It's um . . ." Carl. My stomach jumps. "It's Carl. I called because Ben mentioned you weren't feeling well and you were out yesterday and I thought I would check to see if you are okay. Do you need anything? I mean soup or ginger ale." Did Ben tell him I was throwing up? No, wait. Ben did not know, not for sure. "Anyway, I just thought I would see how you're feeling. And if you're feeling okay maybe you would like to catch a movie this weekend? They're having a Woody Allen marathon at the Cineplex." He rattles off his home phone number and hangs up.

Either Carl got over his office-relationship taboo or he realized rules don't work the way they should sometimes. I hit save and decide to replay it later, to think about it later. Did he pick Woody Allen because he likes him or because he thought I would? Later, I tell myself.

I dump the small stack of library books, half of which I never read, into my mesh tote. The last of the coffee washes the toast crumbs down my throat. Once my teeth are brushed free of breakfast and my hair secured as much as possible, I exit the house. The sky is an odd violet-gray.

My footsteps echo on the library's wide halls. I return my books to the gum-snapping girl with cornrows behind the counter. She scans my card and checks the computer monitor where a record of my borrowing sins glares green against a dark screen. I have to pay seven dollars to restore my good reputation.

The men at the garden-supply store carry everything to my car, though no object weighs more than five pounds. The rumored chivalry of the South still appears, just often enough to prevent me from dismissing it. I turn the car toward home. Beyond the windshield the thunderstorm clouds have passed, streaking the sky with violet streamers.

It takes two trips from my car to Lala's backyard to deposit her supplies. It is less work carrying and shifting items than it is to dissuade Lala from carrying anything. I insist that I am capable of carrying a bag of soil, and no, my back does not hurt, and yes, I know how to lift with my legs.

She gives me lemonade for my efforts. I sip the tart liquid while she looks over her bulbs and tells me what they are and where she will plant them. The string of Latin names lulls me to near sleep. I close my eyes and tilt my face toward the sun. The jays have relocated; Lala's voice drones over the rhythm of a neighbor's water sprinkler and the sporadic barking of the dachshund down the block.

I open my eyes to find Lala bent over her pool, rearranging the rocks. After a few moments she turns, sees I am awake, and smiles. "A few fell," she explains.

"I didn't bring you one today," I say, struck by this fact. I always bring a rock.

She waves away my regret with a hand freckled by sun and age. "You've had a lot on your mind." She settles a black stone more firmly into the crevice of surrounding rocks. Then she rises and sits down opposite me, lowering herself slowly into the seat, as if her legs hurt.

"You won your case. I saw your partner, Ben, on the news."

"Yes."

"You're unhappy?"

"He's going to die," I tell her, turning my eyes to the pool and the goldfish. Two fish swim in small, lazy circles. Did there used to be three?

"I see," she says.

"During sentencing the defense presents evidence of mitigating circumstances. It is a last-ditch effort to convince the jurors not to kill their client. Landry kept talking about Calvin's past: about how his stepfather used to beat him and lock him in closets and I could see this little boy just terrified out of his mind." A soft breeze carries the smell of fabric softener to me. Someone nearby is line-drying clothes. I wrap my arms about my torso.

"He killed two people, right?" Lala rubs the side of her lemonade glass.

"Yes, and I think he ought to pay for that. I do. I just don't think killing him is that price." I sigh, exhausted by rhetoric and emotion. I don't want to talk of this, to think of it, anymore.

"I noticed your gutter is hanging low," she says. I smile in gratitude.

"I know. I need to talk to Mrs. Miller." I do. She is on my kitchen to-do list under "Pick up Lala's garden supplies." I need to ask how much she wants for the house. I need to arrange for an inspection. I need to figure out how to tell my parents I am buying a house in Macon, Georgia. My smile widens, imagining their incredulity. What's wrong with equity? I will ask.

"You going to buy the place?" Her observation startles me. Then I remember mentioning the possibility some time ago, when the idea scared me with its permanence.

"I think so. I like the neighborhood, and the neighbors."

"Ditto," she says.

Her knees pop as she rises from the chair, her hands fisted on the wooden arms for support. "This heat's making me drowsy," she announces. "I think I will go take a nap." She snorts. "Good Lord, but I am truly old. Naptime."

"You stay out here," she says, flapping her hands at me when I stand. "Garden will do you good." I sit, happy to comply. After I hear the door click shut I tilt my head back and stare at the bag of bulbs resting by the stack of garden tools. When will they bloom?

Damn. I meant to ask Lala about the cherry blossom festival. She is sure to know when it begins. I hope to persuade my parents to come. They have to visit sooner or later, especially if I buy the house.

Mom would love the festival. The streets and neighborhoods of Macon burst pink in March as over 275,000 Yoshino cherry trees bloom. The city holds a ten-day festival honoring the beauty of the trees. Amusements, shows, and hot-air balloon rides attract tourists from all over. I could do without the extra people filling parking lots and restaurants, but I do love the trees. Pink and soft and slightly out of focus, they are cotton candy come alive.

Maybe a trip to Lala's garden will make my mother regard my home more favorably. I can argue that I can start a garden of my own in Macon far more easily than in Cambridge, where each square foot of earth sells for roughly half my salary.

A cool breeze makes me shiver. Time to go inside and put on long pants. It is nearly time to get ready for my dinner reservation with Adam and Sonya. I offered to pick them up from the 1842 Inn, where they are staying. I want to call Mrs. Miller before she retires for the evening. I inhale a breath full of sweet air, thick with Lala's flowers and the smoke of grilling meat. Someone is barbecuing. It seems someone always is.

I bid the goldfish good-bye and exit through the wooden gate. As my feet crunch over gravel I stare at the gingham curtains hanging from my windows and practice saying "Welcome to my home." Home. It is a word that does not sound different here than where I came from. A word that means the same everywhere. Home. Home. Home.